CW00973056

32 Caliber

Rhonda Mohammed

Copyright © 2023 by Rhonda Mohammed.

All rights reserved.

No portion of this book may be reproduced in any form without written permission from the publisher or author, except as permitted by U.S. copyright law.

Contents

1

Bring Jim Here

I was in the locker-room of the country-club, getting dressed after the best afternoon of golf I had ever had. I had just beaten Paisley "one-up" in eighteen holes of the hardest kind of sledding.

If you knew Paisley you'd understand just why I was so glad to beat him. He is a most insufferably conceited ass about his golf, for a man who plays as badly as he does; in addition to which he usually beats me. It's not that Paisley plays a better game, but he has a way of making me pull my drive or over-approach just by his confounded manner of looking at me when I am getting ready to play.

We usually trot along about even until we come to the seventh hole—in fact, I'm usually ahead at the seventh—and then conversation does me in. You see, the seventh hole can be played two ways. There's a small clay bank that abuts the green and you can either play around or over it to the hole, which lies directly behind. The real golfers play over with a good mashie shot that lands them dead on the green, but dubs, like Paisley, play around with two easy mid-iron shots. When we get to the place where the choice must be made, Paisley suggests that I go around, which makes me grip my mashie firmly, recall all the things I have read in the little book about how to play a mashie shot, and let drive with all my force, which usually lands me somewhere near the top of the clay bank, where it would take a mountain goat to play the next shot. After that, Paisley and I exchange a few hectic observations and my temperature and score mount to the highest known altitude.

Of course, every now and then, I forget my stance and Paisley long enough to send the ball in a beautiful parabola right on to the green, and when I do—oh, brother!—the things I say to Paisley put him in such a frame of mind that I could play the rest of the course with a paddle and a basket-ball and still beat him. This particular afternoon he had tried to play the seventh hole as it should be played, and though we had both foozled, I had won the hole and romped triumphantly home with the side of pig.

I was gaily humming to myself as I put on my clothes when James Felderson came in. His face was drawn and his mouth was set in a way that was utterly foreign to Jim, whose smile has done more to keep peace in committee meetings and to placate irate members than all other harmonizing agencies in the club put together. There was something unnatural, too, about his eyes, as though he had been drinking.

"Have you seen Helen?" he demanded in a thick voice.

"No. Not to-day," I answered. "What's the matter, Jim? Anything wrong?"

Felderson has been my law partner ever since he married my sister Helen. I had left him at the office just before lunch and he had seemed then as cheerful and unperturbed as usual.

"Helen has gone with Frank Woods!" he burst out, his voice breaking as he spoke.

It took a second for me to grasp the meaning of what he said, then I grabbed him by the shoulder.

"Jim, Jim, what are you saying?"

My sister—left her husband—run off with another man! I had read of such things in stories, but never had I believed that real people, in real life and of real social position, ever so disgraced themselves. Every one knew that Frank Woods had been seeing a lot of Helen, and several close friends had asked me if Jim knew the man's reputation. I had even spoken to Helen, only to be laughed at, and assured that it was the idle gossip of scandal-mongers. That she should have left Jim, darling old Jim, for Frank Woods, or any other man, was unthinkable. Jim sank on a bench and turned a face to me that had grown utterly haggard.

"It's true, Bupps! I found this on the table when I went home to lunch."

He held out a crumpled note written in Helen's rather mannish back-hand.

"Jim,

"It is now ten-thirty. Frank is coming for me at eleven. He has made me realize that, loving him the way I do, I would be doing you a horrible injustice to keep up the wretched pretense of being your wife.

"Had you left any other way open, I would have taken it, but you refused a divorce. I hate to hurt you the way I must, but try to understand and forgive me.

"Helen."

I turned toward Jim. His chin was sunk in his hands. Two men came in from the tennis-courts and nodded as they went by.

"What have you done?" I asked.

He raised his head, and on his face was written incalculable misery.

"Nothing!" he answered, dropping his hands hopelessly. "What can I do, except let them go and get a divorce as soon as possible? It's my fault. After we—quarreled the other night, she asked me to divorce her, and I refused. God, Bupps! If you only knew how much I love her and how hard I've tried to make her love me. And she did love me till Woods came along."

I hurried up my dressing, turning over in my mind the details of Jim's married life. In the light of the latest developments, I realized the painful fact that I was partly to blame myself. Helen hadn't really loved Jim when she married him. Oh, she'd loved him in the same way she'd loved a lot of other men whom she'd been more or less engaged to at one time or another. She had married Jim, because it had been the thing to do that year, to get married; and she realized that Jim loved her more and could give her more than any of the others. Where I came in was that I had urged her to marry Jim because he was the best man in the world and because I wanted him for my brother-in-law.

I remembered now how cold Helen had been, even during their engagement, trumping up almost any excuse to keep from spending an evening alone with the man who was to be her husband. It had made me so hot that I had reproached her even in Jim's presence. My words didn't seem to affect Helen any, but they did affect Jim a lot. He had taken me for a long ride in his car and filled me full of moonshine about how he was unworthy of her and how he would win her love after they were married. I was in such sympathy with him that I tried to believe it true, although I knew Helen as only a younger brother can know a sister. I knew that she had been pampered and petted ever since she was a child; that she had never shown much affection for father and mother, who were her slaves, while toward me, who had insulted and made fun of her, she was almost effusive. With this in mind, I had urged Jim to neglect her, to "treat her rough," but when a man is head-over-heels in love with a girl, what's the good of advice? To tell him to mistreat her was like telling a Mohammedan to spit in the face of the prophet.

They had been married a little over a year when Frank Woods came to Eastbrook on war business for the French Government. He had been in Papa Joffre's Army during part of the mêlée, wore the *Croix de Guerre* with several palms, and could hold a company of people enthralled with stories of his experiences. Whether he had a right to the decorations, or even the uniform, no one was quite sure, but it set off every good point of his massive, well-built frame. He would stand in front of the fire and tell of air-scraps in such a way that, while he never mentioned the hero by name, it was easy to guess that "hero" and Frank Woods were synonymous. He could dance, ride, play any game and shoot better than the best of us, and when he sat at the piano and sang, every man looked at his wife or his fiancée and wondered where the lightning was going to strike. For although he was a very proper young bachelor for months, showing no unseemly interest in women, we all of us, I think, secretly felt that he was setting the stage for a "grand coup."

If he had singled out Helen from the first, he couldn't have played his game better, for his seeming indifference to her loveliness piqued her almost to madness. During the early months of our entrance in the war he was called back to France, and every man in Eastbrook breathed a sigh of relief. There wasn't one of us who could say why we thought him a cad, but just the same, I doubt if there was a father in Eastbrook who would willingly have given his daughter to him. He was too much of the ideal lover to make a good husband. There was something about him, too, that made no man want to claim him as a particular friend, but perhaps it was because we were all jealous.

While most of the younger men of the town were in France, or, like Jim and myself, in a training-camp, Frank Woods came back, and this time there was no mistaking whom he had picked out for his attentions. Until the war was over and Jim home, it was not noticeable, for he was most meticulous in his behavior, but with Jim busy trying to straighten out our tangled practise, Woods lost no time in taking advantage of his opportunities. And there had been opportunities enough, heaven knows, with Jim surrounded by clients, yet trying in his clumsy, lovable way to remonstrate with Helen for seeing so much of Woods. My interference had only increased his opportunities, for the evening I told her what people were saying, she quarreled with Jim, and as a result he threw himself into his work with an energy in which enthusiasm had no part.

All the time these thoughts were running through my head—and they ran much faster than I can set them down—I had been throwing my clothes on, knowing something had to be done, yet what that something was I couldn't for the life of me figure out.

"Come on, Jim!" I said, grabbing him by the arm and pulling him from his dejected position.

"Where to?" he responded wearily.

"First of all, we're going to shut this thing up. *The Sun* would like nothing better than to spread it thick all over the front page of their filthy sheet."

"You're right, old boy! I'd forgotten about the newspapers. It would be horrible for Helen to have her name dragged through the mud."

"I wasn't thinking of Helen," I responded testily, "but a lot of cheap notoriety won't help our law practise any."

All the spirit seemed to have seeped out of his system, so I pushed him into my car, preferring to take the wheel rather than have him drive. I can always think better when I have a steering wheel in my hands, and knowing with what speed Jim drove ordinarily, I didn't care to trust my precious body to him in his overwrought condition.

We were just backing into the drive when one of the servants came running from the club.

"Oh, Mr. Thompson!" he called.

I stopped the car and waited for him to come up.

"What is it?"

"You're wanted on the telephone."

I jumped from the car and started for the club. There were the usual groups of tea-drinkers and bridge-players scattered about on the broad veranda, and it seemed to me, as I ran up the steps, that they all stopped talking and looked at me, I thought, with curiosity, if not with pity. There would be no use shutting up the newspapers if that bunch of gossips were in possession of the scandal.

I hurried to the telephone and slammed the door to the booth, expecting to hear the voice of some reporter demand if there was any truth to the rumor that Mrs. James Felderson had run off with Frank Woods. To my buzzing brain it seemed that the whole world must have heard the news.

"Hello," I called.

"Is that you, Warren?" It was Helen's voice.

"Helen!" I yelled. "For God's sake, where are you?"

"I am at the house. Listen, Warren! Have you seen Jim?"

Her voice sounded faint and strangely uncontrolled.

"Yes—yes," I shouted. "He's here with me now."

"Then bring him here quickly, Warren! Please hurry."

"But, Helen——"

"Don't ask me any questions, please." There was a catch in the voice on the other end of the wire. "I c-can't answer any questions now, but bring Jim, and hurry!"

The receiver clicked and I dashed out of the booth, a thousand questions pounding in my brain. Why was Helen at the house? Had Frank Woods failed to keep his appointment, thinking better of eloping with another man's wife; or, had Helen come to her senses, seen through the thin veneer that covered the cad and the libertine in Frank Woods and returned to her husband for good? Over and above these questions and conjectures and hopes, there was thanksgiving in my heart that the irremediable step had not been taken; that something had intervened to keep scandal and disgrace away from Jim.

There must have been something in my face that told Jim I had been talking to Helen, for he moved into the driver's seat and greeted me with the single question: "Where is she?"

"Home!" I panted, "and drive like the devil!"

I might have saved myself the trouble of the last, for even before I got into the car there was a roar of exhaust and the crunch of grinding gears and we were off down the smooth drive with a speed that quickly brought tears to my eyes and put the fear of God in my heart.

How we ever escaped a smash-up after we got into the city I can't tell to this day, for Jim never once slackened speed. He sat there with jaws set, pumping gas and still more gas into the little car. Thrice I saw death loom up ahead of us, as vehicles approached from side-streets, but with a swerve and a sickening skid, we missed them somehow. Once a street-car and a wagon seemed completely to block the road ahead, but Jim steered for the slender opening and when I opened my eyes we had skinned through, leaving a corpulent and cursing driver far behind. After that I forgot my wretched fear and the blood surged through my veins at the delicious feel of the air as it whipped my cheeks. We turned at last into the long approach to Jim's house and it was then that my heart sank.

Frank Woods' car was standing before the door.

2

Two Men and a Woman

Had Helen been alone, I would have dropped Jim and gone on, knowing that what they had to say to each other was not for outside ears, but when I saw Frank Woods' car there, I felt that a cool head might be needed. There was an ominous set to Jim's shoulders as he walked toward the steps, a sort of drawing in of the head, as though all the muscles in his big frame were tensed. He hesitated a fraction of a second at the door, either to let me catch up with him or because of distaste for the prospective meeting, and we entered the cool dark hall together.

Helen was standing at the entrance to the big living-room, her tall figure erect, her head proudly poised, one graceful arm upraised, with the hand buried in the velvet hangings. She had on a gray traveling-suit, the coat of which lay tossed over the back of a near-by chair. A large patent-leather traveling-case lay beside it. I had expected, from the urgency of the message and the sound of her voice over the telephone, to find Helen agitated, but, except for slight traces of recent tears and a high color, she looked as cool and collected as though she had invited us to tea. Jim, on the other hand, was trembling, his face a pasty white, with great beads of perspiration standing on his forehead.

She motioned us to enter, and I led the way, gripping Jim's hand in passing. Woods was standing by the window, his back to us, and his whole pose so artificial, so expressive of disdain, that I felt the short hair rising along the back of my neck in antagonism. When he heard us, Woods turned with contemptuous deliberation, but when he caught sight of the dumb misery on Jim's face, his own turned a dull crimson. Helen crossed the room and seated herself on the divan, back of which Woods was standing. The whole performance—the place she chose near him, the look she flashed at him as she sat down, showed so completely which of the men she loved, that my heart sank and I lost hope of ever bringing her back to Jim. It was Helen who first spoke.

"You received the note I left this morning?"

Jim moistened his lips once and said, "Yes." The word was barely audible.

"Then there is no need to tell you I have made up my mind to go with Frank."

Her tone was coldly final. Woods had turned and was again gazing out of the window. Jim looked at Helen with the eyes of a hound-dog. My heart ached for him, but there was nothing I could do.

"Why did you come back?" Jim almost whispered, keeping his eyes directly on her face.

"Because I didn't want a scandal." She glanced down at her lap where she was opening and closing a beaded vanity bag. Evidently she was finding the interview harder than she had expected.

"I felt—I hoped that if I could show you definitely and finally that I don't love you, that I am devoted to Frank, your pride, if nothing else, would induce you to give me the divorce for which I asked. That is the reason we decided to come back—so you might make it possible for us to marry without a scandal."

The gross selfishness of the woman—I could hardly think of her as my sister—her cold cruelty, yes, even her damnable beauty, seemed to go to my head and something snapped inside. I couldn't bear the sight of Jim standing there helpless, while these two turned the knife.

"That was very considerate of you," I sneered.

"You keep out of this, Warren!"

"I'm damned if I do," I retorted. "I at least have a brother's right to tell you that a man who will sneak into another's home to make love to his wife, behind his back, and then——"

Woods turned quickly. "That's a lie, and you know it."

Jim put his hand on my shoulder. He knew I was ready to fight.

"Don't, Bupps!"

Suddenly he seemed to straighten into life. From the way he set his jaw, I knew that the old courage, which had won so many cases in the court-room, was back on the job.

"You were quite right, Helen. While I imagine your reason for not wanting a scandal was largely selfish, yet I think that consideration for my position was partly responsible for your return, and for that I thank you. When you asked for a divorce the other night, I didn't realize that your love for me was so entirely dead, or that you had fallen so completely under this man's influence. Under the circumstances, I shall give you a divorce, if only to keep you from taking matters into your own hands. But I shall not do it until I have satisfied myself that your new love is real, that the man is worthy of it. If there is anything in Woods' life that does not bear looking into, I'll find it out; if he has done anything in the past that is likely to hurt you in the future, I shall know it, and you shall know it, too, before you take this irrevocable step."

Woods flushed for a moment when Jim spoke of digging into his past, but he laughed easily and said:

"You're getting a bit melodramatic, aren't you?"

"Better melodrama than tragedy," Jim responded bitterly.

"Helen has told you she doesn't love you, and that she does love me. This morning she was ready to face the scandal of leaving her husband; to go to live with me, to live openly with me, unmarried, until you could get a divorce. That rather answers your first point, doesn't it?"

"It makes me think no better of you, that you should have agreed to such a sacrifice."

"I never expected to win the husband's love at the same time I won his wife's," Woods responded evenly.

Never have I seen murder shine out of a man's eyes as it did out of Jim's at that moment. Each man measured the other across the narrow space, and I longed that the laws of civilization might be swept aside so that the two might tear at each other's throats, for the woman they loved. Both men were powerful, and neither feared the other.

"As to looking up my past," Woods continued, "one might think you were the father of the lady and I a youthful suitor. While I recognize no right of yours to meddle in my affairs, the fact that I was sent to America as the duly accredited agent of the French Government should have some weight. They are not accustomed over there to hiring thugs and cutthroats to carry on their business."

"This is all beside the point," Helen broke in. "May I ask, Jim, where I am going to stay and what I am going to do while you are investigating Frank's past?"

"You are going to stay here."

"Here? But where will you stay?"

"I am going to stay here with you."

Woods came around the divan. "Look here, Felderson! Can't you see Helen doesn't love you, that you've lost—?"

"Keep back!" warned Jim huskily.

"She can't stay here with you. She's no more your wife than if she had never married you. Do you think I'll allow her to stay in this house, forced to endure your attentions—?"

"Who are you to say what you will or won't allow?" Jim roared, his eyes blazing. "You came into my house as my guest and stole my most precious possession. Get out before I kill you!"

Woods' face was white. For one minute I felt sure the two men would settle matters then and there. Suddenly he turned and said: "Come, Helen!"

"She stays here!" Jim cried.

Helen had arisen from the divan when the two men came together. Now she stepped forward.

"I'm going with Frank. We came back here more for your sake than our own. We tried to give you a chance to do the decent thing, but I might have known you wouldn't. With all your protestations of love for me, when I ask you to do the one thing that would show that love, the one thing that would make me happy, you not only refuse, but you insult the man who means everything in the world to me. If I had ever loved you in my life, what you have just said would have made me hate you. As I never loved you, I despise and loathe you now."

She started to pass him, but he grabbed her by the shoulders. His face was white and drawn and his eyes were the eyes of a madman. He lifted her up bodily and almost threw her on the divan, crying, "By God! You stay here!"

Jim turned just as Woods rushed and with a mighty swing to the side of the head, sent him crashing into the corner. Dazed as he was, he half struggled to his feet, and when I saw him reach beneath his coat, I sprang on him and wrenched the revolver from his hand.

Disheveled and half-stupefied, he rose and glared at us like an angry bull. Slowly he straightened his tie and brushed back his hair. He glanced over at Helen, who was sobbing on the sofa.

"Two of you—eh? A frame-up." All the hatred in the world gleamed in his eyes, as he looked at Jim. "If you don't let Helen come to me, Felderson, I'll kill you; so help me God, I'll kill you!" Then he picked up his coat and hat and walked out of the room.

Jim went slowly to the door and into the hall. He looked tired and old. I heard the outer door slam behind Frank Woods and a motor start. Then I went out to Jim.

3

I Could Kill Him

I was on my way back to Jim's after having gone home to change my clothes. Jim had asked me to stay with him that evening and, to tell the truth, I was glad to do it, partly because of the threat Woods had made and partly because of the way Helen looked at Jim when she passed us in the hall on the way to her bedroom. Being a lawyer, I have naturally made a pretty close study of character, and if I ever saw vindictiveness on the face of any human, it was on Helen's at that moment.

I said nothing about the affair to mother while I was home, for she has been very frail ever since my father's death and I thought there was no use in needlessly upsetting her. There would be plenty of time to discuss the matter after Helen left Jim.

Again and again I recalled the struggle of the afternoon and again and again, Helen's face, distorted with anger, reappeared. Finally I decided to drive the car over to Mary Pendleton's and ask her to come spend the night with Helen. In her overwrought, hysterical condition, Helen was capable of doing almost anything.

Mary has been like a second sister to me. She really cares nothing for me, except in a sisterly way, but we have been together, so much so and so long that Eastbrook gossips have given up speculating whether we are engaged. I'd marry her in a minute, or even less, if she would have me, but Mary insists on treating me like a kid; calls my crude attempts at love-making "silly tosh and flub-dub," which makes the going rather difficult. She was bridesmaid to Helen and is the one person, besides myself, who can influence her in the least, so I felt that her presence would add ballast to our wildly tossing domestic craft. Needless to say, my own lack of self-control during the afternoon had been as unexpected as it was disappointing, but when it comes to anything that concerns Jim, I'm not responsible.

I rang the bell and Mary, herself, came to the door, looking radiant as usual.

"Hello, Buppkins!" She greeted me with that detestable nick-name she has used since I wore rompers. "Aren't you trying for a record or something? This is twice you've called on me this month."

"Mary, I'm in trouble."

"Is the poor 'ittle boy in trouble and come to Auntie Mary to tell her all about it?" she sing-songed, making a little moue, as though she was talking to her pet cat.

"Cut it, Mary!" I said. "I'm really in trouble."

"What is it, Bupps?"

"Helen ran off with Frank Woods to-day."

"Heavens, Bupps!"—she was serious enough now.—"Where did they go?"

"They went, but they came back. Helen's home with Jim. They tried to force him to give Helen a divorce. There was an awful fight and Woods swore that he would kill Jim unless he let Helen go. But put on your hat and coat and get your things. Helen needs you with her. I'll tell you the rest on the way over."

"I'll be with you in a second," she called, running up-stairs.

When Mary was snuggled down beside me in the car—and she does snuggle the best of any girl I ever knew—I told her everything, not forgetting the part where I wrenched the gun away from Woods.

"Goodness, Bupps! I bet you were scared," she commented, her eyes twinkling.

"Frankly, I didn't know what I was doing, or I would never have had the nerve," I laughed. "But, lord! I feel sorry for Jim."

Mary's face clouded over.

"So do I, Bupps, but any one could have seen it coming. Jim was too good to her. As much as I like Helen, I will say that the only kind of husband she deserves is a brute who would beat her. That's the only kind she can love. I was with her the night before her wedding, and she confessed then that if Jim were only cruel or indifferent to her, just once, she thought she could love him to death. The only reason Helen cares for you and me, was because we never paid any particular attention to her when she acted up and pouted. That is why she is mad about Frank Woods. When he came to Eastbrook, he treated her as though she didn't exist."

"And if Jim were cruel to her now, do you think she would go back to him?" I asked.

Mary shook her head. "No, it's different now. If Jim were cruel to her, she would probably hate him all the more for it."

"Proving the incomprehensibility of woman," I jeered.

"Proving the flumdability of flapdoodle," Mary responded. "If you men only put one little thought into giving a woman what she wants, instead of giving her what you think she ought to want; if you kept as up-to-date in your love-making as you do in your law practise, women wouldn't be the incomprehensible riddle you always make them out to be."

"Well, why don't you tell us what you want?" I asked.

"Silly! That would spoil it all, don't you see? Besides we aren't sure just what we want ourselves."

My spirits, which had risen considerably during our conversation, dropped with a slump when Jim's big house loomed up ahead. Already, something of the unhappiness within seemed to have added a more somber touch to the outside. Have you noticed how you can tell from the face of a house what kind of life the inhabitants lead? Happiness or misery, health or sickness, riches or poverty all show as though the walls were saturated from the admixture of life within.

I sent Mary up-stairs to see Helen, while I went into the drawing-room in search of Jim, but there was no one there except Wicks, the butler, who was lighting a fire, for, though it was only the last of September, the nights were chilly. I snatched up the evening paper to see if by any chance a hint of the scandal had crept into print. I felt sure that, as matters stood, they would not dare to put in anything definite, but *The Sun* has a nasty way of writing all around a scandal, so that, while the persons involved are readily recognized, they are quite helpless as far as redress is concerned.

I noticed that Wicks had taken an infernally long time to start the fire. Although it was burning merrily, he still puttered about, brushing up the chips and rearranging the blower and tongs. When Wicks hangs about he usually has a question on his mind that he wants answered, and he takes that means of letting you know it. I decided not to notice him but to force him to come out in the open and ask, for once, a straightforward question. From the fire, he moved to the table and straightened the magazines and books, glancing now and then in my direction, trying to catch my eye, but I buried myself more deeply than ever in the paper. When he finally stepped back of my chair, human nature could stand his puttering no longer, so I laid down *The Sun*, and turned to him.

"Well, Wicks, what do you want?" I snapped.

Wicks looked at me with the expression of a small boy caught sticky-handed in the jam-closet.

"Nothing, sir!—that is—er—nothing." He turned and started from the room.

"Come here, Wicks!" I called. "I know when you hang around a room unnecessarily, as you have been doing for the last ten minutes, that you have something on your mind. Now, out with it."

"I was merely going to arsk, sir, hif I 'ad better begin lookin' arfter another place, sir?"

That was an extraordinary question. Wicks had been with the Feldersons ever since they were married.

"What put that idea into your head, Wicks?"

He was far more confused than I had ever seen him.

"Meanin' no disrespect, sir, and I don't mean to be hinquisitive about what doesn't concern me, but I couldn't 'elp 'earin' a bit of what took place this arfternoon, sir."

Good lord! I'd forgotten there might have been other witnesses to the scene of the afternoon besides myself.

"Do the other servants know about this, Wicks?"

"Hi think they do, sir, seein' as 'ow Mrs. Felderson 'as been actin' and talkin' so queer."

"What do you mean?" I demanded.

Wicks struggled for composure. The subject was evidently most distasteful to his conservative and conventional British nature.

"Hit was Annie, Mrs. Felderson's maid, sir, that hupset the servants. W'en she came down from hup-stairs, she said as 'ow Mrs. Felderson was a ragin' and a rampagin' around 'er room, sayin' that if Mr. Felderson didn't give 'er a divorce, she would do violence to 'im, sir."

"Did Annie hear her say that?" I questioned.

"She says so, sir."

The whole thing was so monstrous that I gasped. For this awful dime-novel muck to be tumbled into the middle of my family was too sickening. My sister, running away from her husband with another man and now threatening, in the hearing of the servants, to kill him, unless he gave her a divorce, disgusted me with its cheap vulgarity. I hid, as best I could, the tempest that was brewing inside me.

"Wicks, Mrs. Felderson is not well. Tell the servants that she is greatly depressed over an accident that happened to a friend. At the present time, she is so upset over that, she really doesn't know what she is saying. Quiet them in some way, Wicks! And tell Annie to stay with Mrs. Felderson!"

"Very good, sir." He started to leave.

"And, Wicks—"

"Yes, sir."

"There is no need of your looking for another place."

"Yes, sir. Thank you, sir!"

Wicks departed and I was left to my gloomy thoughts. Helen must be brought to her senses. Mary and I must work, either to bring her back to Jim, or, if that prove hopeless, to see that the divorce was hurried as much as possible. The very thought of having Mary along with me, with her inexhaustible fund of God-given humor and common sense, gave me a vast amount of comfort and confidence.

At this point, Jim came in. He had had a bath and a shave and had put on a dinner-coat, looking a lot more fit to grapple with his troubles than he had the last time I had seen him. Only in his eyes did he show the shock he'd received that day.

"Communing with yourself in the dark, Bupps?"—his voice was natural and easy.

"Yes," I sighed, "I've been trying to see a way out of this mess."

Jim lit a cigarette and threw himself into a chair. For a few moments he puffed in silence, taking deep inhalations and blowing the smoke against the lighted tip, so that it showed all the rugged, strength of his superb head.

"What would you say, Bupps, if I told you everything would come out all right?"

"And Helen stay with you?" I asked incredulously.

"And Helen stay with me," he repeated calmly.

"Of her own free will?"

"Of her own free will," he answered.

"I should say that the events of the day had addled your brain and that you are a damned inconsiderate brother-in-law to try to make a fool of me."

"I mean it, Bupps," he said quietly.

"What do you mean?" I demanded.

"That everything will come out all right," he smiled.

"But how, man?" His complacency almost drove me wild.

"Bupps, have you noticed how much money Woods has been spending around here—his extravagant way of living? Where do you think that money comes from?"

"His contracts with the French Government," I replied.

"But I happen to know he didn't land those contracts. That's the reason he beat it so suddenly when we got into the war." He tossed his cigarette into the fire.

"His salary from the French, then. They must have paid him some kind of salary."

"Have you never heard what ridiculously small salaries the French Government pays its officers?"

It was true that Woods could never have lived as he did on ten times the salary of a French captain.

"His own private fortune then," I suggested.

"Ah! There's the point! If he has a private fortune, then my whole case falls to pieces. That's what I've got to find out. Woods has been playing for a big stake, and I think he has been playing with other people's money. Did you notice how he flushed this afternoon when I suggested looking into his private affairs? It was the veriest accident—I was stalling for time—but when I saw him color up I knew I'd touched a sore spot. No, Bupps, I don't think Woods has a private fortune."

"But even if you show him up as worthless, will Helen come back to you, Jim?"

The color came to his face and he laughed with a queer twist to his mouth.

"Am I as horrible as all that, Bupps?"

His words brought a lump to my throat. I went over to him and almost hugged him.

"Jim, you're such a peach—dammit all—"

I heard a light step behind me.

"Oh, Bupps!" laughed Mary, "if you'd only make love to me in that ardent fashion, I'd drag you to the altar by your few remaining hairs."

I stood up, blushing in spite of myself. She can always make me feel that whatever I am doing is either stupid or foolish.

"Dinner is served, and I'm starving. Come on, people!" she announced, leading the way to the dining-room.

"Where's Helen?" I asked.

"She's not coming down. She has a slight headache," Mary answered, giving me a warning look. "I am delegated to be lady of the manor this evening." She looked so adorable as she curtsied to us that I felt an almost uncontrollable impulse to grab her in my arms and smother her with kisses, but remembering what she had done to me once when I yielded to impulse, I refrained.

When we sat down to the table, Helen's empty place threatened to cast a gloom over the party, so Mary told Wicks to remove it.

"It's too much like Banquo's ghost," she whispered, laughing merrily at Jim.

"Speaking of ghosts," said Jim turning to me, "I hear the labor people are asking the governor to pardon Zalnitch."

"A lot of good it will do them," I responded. "If ever a man deserved hanging, he does."

"I know, but labor is awfully strong now, and with the unsettled social conditions in the state, a bigger man than Governor Fallon might find it expedient to let Zalnitch off."

"Who is Zalnitch? Don't think I've met the gentleman," Mary said.

"He's the Russian who was supposed to be the ring-leader of the gang that blew up the Yellow Funnel steamship piers in 1915," I explained.

"Do you mean to say he hasn't been hanged yet?"

"Yes!" Jim answered. "And what's more, I'm afraid he's going to be pardoned."

"Not really, Jim?" I queried.

"Yes! I'm almost sure of it. Fallon is a machine man before everything else, although he was elected on a pro-American ticket. They are threatening to do all kinds of things to him, just as they threatened me, unless Zalnitch goes free, and I think Fallon is afraid of them, not physically perhaps, but politically. He wants reelection."

Jim had helped the prosecuting attorney convict Zalnitch; in fact it was Jim's work more than anything else that had sent the Russian to prison. At the time, Jim had received a lot of threatening letters, just as every other American who denounced the Germans before we entered the war had received them. Nothing had come of it, of course, and after we went in, the whole matter dropped from public attention. Zalnitch had been sent to prison, but his friends had worked constantly for commutation of his sentence. With labor's new power, due to the fear of Bolshevism, they were again bringing influence to bear on the governor.

Wicks had removed the soup plates and was bringing in the roast, when Annie appeared. The girl was both frightened and angry.

"Mr. Felderson?"

Jim looked up. "What is it, Annie?"

"Will you come up-stairs, please, sir?"

Mary pushed back her chair, "I'll go, Jim."

"It's Mr. Felderson that's wanted," Annie said with just a touch of asperity.

"Yes, you two better stay here and amuse each other," said Jim.

"Bupps, you carve!"

"If Bupps carves, I'm *sure* to be amused," laughed Mary.

Jim left, and I went around to his place. If there is one thing I do more badly than another, it is carving. At home it's done in the kitchen, but Jim takes great pride in the neatness and celerity with which he separates the component parts of a fowl and so insists on having the undissected whole brought to the table.

"What is it to-night?" Mary asked as I eyed my task with disfavor.

"Roast duck." I tried to speak casually.

"Wait, Bupps, while Wicks lays the oilcloth and I get an umbrella."

"Smarty!" I responded, grabbing my tools firmly, "you wait and see! I watched Jim the last time he carved one of these and I know just how it's done."

I speared for the duck's back, but the fork skidded down the slippery side of the bird and spattered a drop of gravy in front of me.

"I'm waiting and seeing," Mary chided.

"Well, you wanted some gravy, didn't you?"

"Yes, but on my plate, please."

This time I placed the tines of the fork carefully on the exact middle of the duck's breast and gently pushed, giving some aid and comfort with my knife. The little beast eased over on the platter an inch or two.

"The thing's still alive," I exclaimed, getting mad.

"If you'll let me have full control, I'll carve it for you," Mary spoke up.

"Come on, then," I responded, gladly relinquishing my place. With a deftness and ease that could only be explained by the fact that the duck was ready and willing to be carved, she removed the legs and then demolished the bird altogether.

There was the sound of voices raised in altercation up-stairs, the slamming of a door and the patter of feet rapidly descending the steps. The next moment Helen burst into the room. She was fully dressed for going out and was pinning on her hat with spiteful little jabs.

"Will you take me home, Warren?"

Mary left me and went over to her.

"What has happened, Helen?"

"Oh, I can't stay here another minute. It is bad enough to have to stay in the same house with a man you loathe, but when a husband bribes his wife's servants to spy on her and watch over her as though she were a dangerous lunatic—"

Her eyes were blazing. Mary put her arm around her and tried to quiet her.

"Helen, dear, you don't know how ridiculous that is. No one is spying on you."

Helen tore herself away.

"That's right, stand up for him! You're all against me, I know. The only reason Warren brought you here, was to try to talk me into staying with him. Well, I won't, you understand? I won't! I hate him! I could kill him! If you won't take me home, Warren, I'll go alone." She was almost hysterical.

"Have you thought what this would do to mother?" I asked. "She doesn't know you've quarreled with Jim. If she found out you were contemplating a divorce, it would kill her. You know how weak she is."

I heard Jim's heavy tread coming downstairs.

"Can I stay with you, Mary?" Big tears stood in Helen's eyes and she seemed on the verge of a complete breakdown.

"Of course, Honey-bunch!" Mary responded, kissing her and leading her into the drawing-room. "Just go in there and lie down while I get my things."

As Helen walked from the room, Jim came in. Mary turned toward us, looked us over for the briefest moment and whispered, "You men are brutes!" As she ran up-stairs, Jim gazed after her. That same gray look had come back into his face.

"I guess we are," he said, shaking his head, "but I don't know how or why."

I patted him on the shoulder and went for my coat. Whether he realized it or not, I knew Helen would never come back to him.

I went out to the car and turned on the lights. A white moon was sailing through a sky cluttered with puffy clouds, its soft radiance bathing the house and grounds in mellow loveliness. It all seemed so remote from the sordid quarrel inside that its beauty was enhanced by the contrast. Here was a night when the whole world should be in love. Nature herself conspired to that end. And yet, there were thousands of men and women who were so forgetful of everything except their own petty differences that they turned their backs to the beauty around them, in order to try to hurt each other.

As Helen and Mary came out of the door, I climbed into the car and said to myself, "Damn men, damn women, damn everything!"

4

The Worst Happens

I was late getting down to the office the next morning, for I had gone back to Jim's and talked till all hours. It seemed that my instructions to Wicks, to tell Annie to stay with Helen, had been taken quite literally by that estimable pair, for when Helen had told the girl to leave she had refused, saying that Mr. Felderson had ordered her to stay. That was what had precipitated the quarrel.

Even when I left Jim, to go to bed, I had heard him walking back and forth in his room, and once during the night, I heard him shut his door. Thinking perhaps he might want me with him, I went to his door and knocked. Jim was untying his shoes and explained that, unable to sleep, he had gone out for a walk. The clock on the mantel-piece showed half past four.

In spite of the fact he had practically no sleep the night before, he was down at his usual hour, nine o'clock, and when I went into his office to see him, there was no sign of fatigue on his face.

"Any news?" I inquired.

"This may interest you," and he tossed over the morning paper folded to an article on the first page.

ZALNITCH FREED

GOVERNOR FALLON PARDONS MAN IMPLICATED IN YELLOW PIER EX-PLOSION

Prisoner Upon Release Makes Terrific

Indictment Against Those Responsible for

His Imprisonment

I glanced hurriedly down the long article. One paragraph in particular caught my eye. It was part of a quotation from Zalnitch's "speech" to the reporters.

"Those who were responsible for my imprisonment may well regret the fact that justice has at last been given me. I shall not rest until I lay before the working classes the extent to which the processes of law can be distorted in this state, and rouse them to overthrow and drive out those who have the power of depriving them of their rights and their liberty. I shall not rest until I see a full meed of punishment brought to those who have punished me and hundreds like me. Their money and their high position will not help them to escape a just retribution."

"It looks as though our friend was going to have a very restless time," I commented, after reading the passage aloud to Jim.

"'Vengeance is mine,' saith Zalnitch." Jim's eyes twinkled.

"You're not afraid of him, are you, Jim?" I asked.

"No more now than ever, Bupps."

His face suddenly clouded over. "Wouldn't it clear the air, though, if they did carry out their funny little threats and put me out of the way? When I think of some of the things Helen has said to me during the last month, I almost wish they would."

"That sounds weak and silly," I scoffed; "not a bit like you, Jim. Cheer up! Give Helen a divorce and let her go! She's not worth all this heartache."

Jim sat for a moment thinking. "You don't know what this has done to me, Bupps. It's not as though divorcing Helen would straighten the whole matter out. Ever since I've known Helen I've—idolized her—foolishly, perhaps. She has been the one big thing worth working for; the thing I've built my whole life around. I've got to fight for her, Bupps. I can't let her smash my ideals all to pieces. I've got to make her live up to what I've always believed her to be."

The tone of the man, the dead seriousness of his words, made me want to disown Helen and then kill Woods. I left the room with my eyes a bit misty and did my best, in the case I was working on, to forget.

For two days I was kept so busy I hardly saw Jim except when I had to go into his office for papers, or to consult an authority. I was trying to win a case against the L. L. & G. railroad, and though I knew my client could never pay me a decent fee, even if I should win, I was pitted against some of the best lawyers in the state, and was anxious for the prestige that a verdict in my favor would give me. The case was going my way, or seemed to be, but the opposition was fighting harder every day, so that I had time for little else than food, sleep and work. Frank Woods had apparently left town, either on business or to give Helen a clear field to influence Jim. Helen was still at Mary's, and her presence on a visit there was so natural that it hid her separation from Jim better than if she had gone home to mother.

I was just leaving for court one morning when Jim called me into his office. There was a gleam of triumph in his eyes and his whole attitude was one of cheerful excitement.

"Have you a minute, Bupps?"

"Only a minute, Jim. This is the day of days for me."

There were several letters and telegrams lying on the table. Jim pointed exultantly to them and cried: "I've got him, Bupps! There is enough evidence there to send Woods up for twenty years. I wouldn't have used such underhand methods against any one else, against anything but a snake, but I had to win, I had to win!"

I rushed to the table and rapidly scanned one of the telegrams.

"You've started at the wrong end, but it doesn't matter. Frank Woods has used the money entrusted him by the French Government to gamble with. He counted on the contracts with the International Biplane people to bring him clean and leave him a comfortable fortune besides. The end of the war and the wholesale cancellation of government contracts killed that. To cover his deficits, he borrowed from the Capitol Loan and Trust, and they are hunting for their money now."

"How did you find all this out, Jim?" I demanded breathlessly.

"From friends, good friends, Bupps. Men who knew that if I asked for this unusual information, I had need of it and that I wouldn't abuse their confidence."

"And now that you've got it, what are you going to do with it?"

"I have sent messages to Woods, to his apartment, to the club and to the International plant, saying that I want to see him. I know he is working like the devil to get the contracts to furnish the government with mail planes for next year. If he gets that contract, he may possibly pull through, for the bank would probably extend his credit, but if knowledge of his illegal use of the money entrusted to him by the French Government ever gets out, he knows it's the stripes without the stars for him."

"Be careful when you meet him, Jim," I warned. "He'll go to the limit, you know, to save himself."

"He's all front, Bupps; just like Zalnitch. I'll give him three days to straighten out his affairs and get away. If he hasn't left by then, I'll put all the evidence I have into the hands of the Capitol Loan and Trust."

"Are you going to tell Helen about this?" I asked.

Jim pondered a moment. "I haven't decided that yet. If I was sure Woods would go away without any trouble, I think I'd leave her in ignorance; but he might use her to save himself."

"How do you mean?"

"I'm not so blind I can't see that Helen's infatuated with the man. If he is blackguard enough to ask her again to go with him, I think she would go, and that would pretty effectively tie my hands."

"You mean that for Helen's sake you wouldn't prosecute Woods?" I demanded. "That's stupid sentimentality."

"It's for Helen's sake that I'm doing *all* this," Jim insisted. "Don't think for a moment I would stop the prosecution just because she was with him. The reason my hands would be tied is because Helen's money would pay his obligations."

"Helen's money?" I laughed. "Helen hasn't as much as I have."

Jim flushed. "Helen is quite a wealthy woman, Bupps. When I went into the army I wanted to leave Helen perfectly easy in a financial way while I was gone, so I transferred all my railroad stock to her, so that she might draw the interest. I haven't asked her for it since I came home, because, in the light of our recent differences, I was afraid she might think I didn't trust her."

"And do you suppose Woods knows that?"

"Of course he knows it!" Jim burst out. "She must have told him. Why do you suppose he played around so long before deciding to make love to Helen? Oh, it's all so simple and clear to me now that I wonder at my stupidity."

I glanced at my watch.

"Good lord, Jim! You've almost made me lose my case. I have only three minutes to get to the court-house. Hold up the climax until I get back, if you can."

I jumped for the elevator and rushed to my appointment, getting there just in time. The news of the morning had so raised my spirits that I was filled with an immense enthusiasm. Everything went my way. My summing up was a masterpiece of logic, if I do say so myself, and my client received a substantial judgment.

There is no moment sweeter in a young lawyer's life than when another lawyer, of big reputation, congratulates him on his conduct of a case. My cup was filled to overflowing, and I must confess I had little thought for Jim's affairs when I lunched that day with Stevenson and McGuire, councils for the L. L. & G. The prognostications that they made for my future were so exaggerated that a bigger man than I might well have been excused for increased head and chest measurements.

At half past two I went back to the office to announce the good news to Jim. I had made up my mind before luncheon to spend the afternoon on the links in honor of my victory, but the clouds, which had been heavy during the morning, by two o'clock opened up a steady drizzle. Jim was at his desk when I came in bringing the glad tidings. He got up and gripped my hand.

"Good boy, Bupps! I knew you'd do it. Thank the Lord your affairs are going well anyway."

"Has something happened since I've been out?" I asked.

"Yes. The First National telephoned about eleven o'clock saying that Helen wanted to borrow quite a large sum of money on her railroad stock and asking if I knew about it. They thought the money was probably for me and they wanted to ask if I'd be willing to wait a few days."

"How much was it?"

"Fifty thousand dollars."

"Is the stock worth that much, Jim?"

"Yes," said Jim seriously, "the stock is worth twice that. That's why I have to go slow. She could sell that stock for fifty thousand at any broker's in five minutes."

I whistled. "Gee! Fifty thousand. Woods must have asked her for it because he knew you were after him."

"It's open warfare now. I told the bank I knew what the money was for and that it would cause no inconvenience to me to have them hold up the loan for a few days. In fact I asked Sherwood, the cashier, to wait until he saw me before making the loan."

Just then the telephone rang. Jim answered it.

"Hello—Yes—Woods?—Where are you now?" He listened a moment. "I understand—Eight-thirty promptly?—I'll be there—Yes, I understand—I'll be there."

He hung up the receiver and looked at me with twinkling eyes.

"The shoe is beginning to pinch, Bupps. That was Woods. He asks me to meet him alone this evening at the country-club, at eight-thirty promptly. Says he wants to see me urgently on business that concerns us both."

"Did he ask you to come alone?"

"Yes. He distinctly said that I was to come alone and be prompt."

"Jim," I argued, "you can't go out there alone to meet that man. It's too infernally dangerous."

"There's no danger, Bupps; but I'm not going alone. Helen is going with me."

He opened the bottom drawer of his desk and pulled out a leather portfolio, into which he put all the letters and telegrams that were scattered about his desk.

"I'm going to prove to Helen, in his presence, what kind of man he is; that he loves her only for the money I gave her, and to save his yellow hide. I'm going to tear out of her heart all the affection she ever had for him. I think, after that, she will not only come back to me, but she will love me all the more for having known Frank Woods. No matter how badly a leg or an arm may be shattered, a quick, clean operation may cause the parts to grow together again, stronger than they were before. I think I win, Bupps."

"Still, I believe you ought to carry a gun, in case he gets nasty."

"I will, if you like," he responded; "but I won't use it, no matter what happens."

I left the office, vaguely disquieted with the thought of Jim going out to the club to face a man as dangerous and desperate as Frank Woods. When a fellow of his standing sees the penitentiary looming up in his foreground he's capable of anything. Helen, herself, in the crazed condition I had seen her the other night, was an added element of danger. I didn't like the looks of the situation any way I turned.

I climbed into my car and drove slowly through the wet slippery streets. The windshield was so covered with rain-drops that I lowered it to see the better, and the autumn rain, beating into my face, soon swept away my gloomy forebodings. After all, no man was going to stick his neck into the hangman's noose, no matter how eager he was for revenge. This was the twentieth century, in which no man could deliberately flout the law. Frank

Woods would never have invited Jim to a "rendezvous" so public as the country-club, if he planned mischief. When he found out how much Jim knew, realizing the game was up, he would leave town quietly. Helen certainly would shake Woods when she learned of his dishonesty and trickery. Surely, no woman with Helen's pride could learn how she had been duped without hating the man who duped her.

I stopped at the University Union and found the card room well filled with bridge players. The rainy afternoon had driven the golfers to cards, and as one of the men, Terry O'Connel, was on the point of leaving, I took his place. I played till seven and then started home to dinner. The rain had stopped and a fresh chilly wind was rippling the pools in the streets and rapidly drying the sidewalks. The prospect of a cold blustery evening made me look forward with pleasure to the warm comfort of my study, and a good book.

I had just finished a solitary dinner—mother being confined to her room—and had settled down in dressing gown and slippers before my cheerful fire, when the telephone rang. I put down my book and tried to think of some excuse for staying home, in case it was my bridge-playing friends of the afternoon wanting me to come back to the club. A strange voice called from the other end of the wire.

"Mr. Thompson?"

"Yes."

"There has been an accident to your brother-in-law's car."

"What?—Where?—Who is this talking?" I shouted breathlessly.

"This is Captain Wadsworth of the North District Police Station speaking. Your brother-in-law had a very bad accident with his car at the second bridge on the Blandesville Road. Both Mr. and Mrs. Felderson were pretty badly injured."

"Where are they now?" I gasped, fear clutching at my throat.

"They have been taken to St. Mary's Hospital."

I slammed down the receiver and tore into my clothes. I ran out to the car and drove through the dark wet streets regardless of speed laws. From out the gray gloom, the heavy bulk and lighted windows of St. Mary's loomed just ahead. I ran up the steps and went at once to the office. Three nurses were standing there talking.

"Can you tell me where they have taken Mr. and Mrs. Felderson?"

"Were they the people in the automobile accident?"

I nodded my head.

One of the nurses led me to a large room on the second floor. As we neared the door a young intern, so the nurse told me, came out. He was thoughtfully polishing his glasses.

"I am Warren Thompson, Mr. Felderson's brother-in-law," I explained.

"Can you tell me how badly Mr. and Mrs. Felderson were hurt?"

He put his glasses back on his nose and looked at me sympathetically.

"Mr. Felderson is dead, and Mrs. Felderson is dying," he said.

5

ACCIDENT OR MURDER

Have you ever had the whole world stop for you? Well, that's what happened when that young intern told me that Jim was dead. I must have been half mad for a few moments, at least they said I acted that way.

Sometimes, tragic news deadens the senses, like the brief numbness that follows the sudden cutting off of a limb, the pain not manifesting itself until some time afterward. But with me, the fact of Jim's death clawed and tore at the very foundation of my brain. It stamped itself into my sensibilities with such crushing force that I writhed under the burden of its bitter actuality. I felt as though I, myself, had died and my spirit, snatched from the brilliant, airy sunlight of life, had been plunged into the hammering emptiness of hell. "Jim is dead—big, happy, kind-hearted Jim is dead" ached through my brain.

They gave me something to drink—ammonia, I think—and my whirling head began to clear.

"Can I see Mrs. Felderson?" I asked the intern. It was he who had given me the ammonia.

"I'm afraid not," he replied. "She is being prepared for the operating table."

"There is a chance, then, of her being saved?" I clutched at his arm.

He slowly shook his head. "One chance in a thousand only, I'm afraid. There was severe concussion of the brain and a slight displacement of one of the cranial vertebra. Luckily, Doctor Forbes is here, and if any one can save her, he can." He got up from his seat beside me. "Now, Mr. Thompson, I advise you to go home and get a good night's rest. You can do nothing here, and the next few days are bound to be a great strain."

"You will telephone me at once the result of the operation?" I asked quickly.

"I wouldn't count too much on the operation," he said kindly, "but I will let you know."

He turned and walked back toward Helen's room. Just then the door was opened and there appeared a sort of elongated baby-cab, without a top. On this wheeling table was a still white bundle, from which a stifled moan escaped now and then. Shaken with terror and nausea, I ran for the stairs and did not stop until I got into my car and was racing away.

As I drove, my brain cleared and I remembered that there were others to whom the tragedy was almost as vital as to myself and who ought to be informed. I stopped at a corner drug store and called up Mary. Mother should not be told until a physician could assure me she was strong enough to stand the shock.

Mary was wonderfully sympathetic and tender, not voluble the way some women would have been. She asked me if I had been to the scene of the accident, and when I told her I was just going, she asked me if I wanted her with me. As it was after ten o'clock and the rain had begun again, I told her "No," and added that I'd come to see her in the morning.

When I left the telephone-booth the drug clerk stared at me inquisitively.

"You look all fagged out," he said frankly.

"I'm not feeling very well," I replied, struggling into my rain-coat.

"Better let me give you somethin' to fix you up," he suggested. I acquiesced, and he went to the shelf and shook some white powder into a glass. Then he put some water with it and it phizzed merrily. I drank it at a gulp and, climbing into the car, started for the second bridge on the Blandesville Road.

The drink braced me up and as I drove I began to recall the events of the last few days, and for the first time to wonder if they had any connection with the tragedy. Captain Wadsworth had told me it was an accident. Could Frank Woods have been in any way responsible? No, certainly not, for Helen had been in the car, and he surely would never have done anything to put her life in jeopardy. *But Woods didn't know that she was there.*

He had told Jim to come out alone; had insisted on it, in fact. It was *Jim's* idea to bring Helen with him.

My heart was doing a hundred revolutions to the minute. Now that I had hit on this idea, every fiber of my being cried out that Frank Woods was in some way responsible. I tried to urge my car to more speed. The wreck would surely tell me something. I determined to hunt every inch of ground around the place for a clue. Woods would have to prove to me that he had nothing to do with the accident before I'd believe him innocent.

I drove up the long hill overlooking the little bridge that had suddenly assumed such a tragic significance in my life. It lies at the bottom of the hill, about half-way between the city and the country-club and on the loneliest stretch of the entire road. There are no houses about; the city not having grown that far out and the soil being entirely unsuitable for farming. In fact, there are only one or two large trees near by, to break the desolate expanse, the vegetation consisting mostly of thorny bushes springing from the rocky soil. There have been several accidents at the bridge, for its narrowness is deceiving and it is impossible for two autos to pass. Motorists, going to the club, usually let their cars out on the long hill and if another car, coming around the bend from the opposite direction, reaches the bridge at the same time, only skilful driving and good brakes can avoid a smash-up. The matter has been brought to the attention of the authorities several times, but nothing has ever been done, either to widen the bridge or to warn automobilists of the danger.

As I reached the top of the hill, I saw that two automobiles had stopped at the bottom, and, noticing that their lights blinked as people passed back and forth in front of them, I was convinced that a small crowd had gathered, probably out of curiosity. I slowed up as I neared the spot and came to a stop at the side of the road. A motorcycle cop walked up to my car.

"Inspector Robinson, sir?"

"No," I answered, "I am Warren Thompson, brother-in-law of Mr. Felderson, who had the accident. How did it happen, do you know, Sergeant?"

"It was the fault of the bridge again, sir. I've told the chief that something ought to be done. This is the third accident in six months. We've been trying to find the other car."

"What other car?" I asked.

"The car that made Mr. Felderson take the ditch," he explained. "He must have been driving fast—he usually did; many's the time I've had to warn him—and must have seen that the other car would meet him at the bridge. He stopped too quick, skidded off the road and turned over into the creek."

I shuddered as I pictured the scene. One of the automobiles turned around and the lights picked out the upturned wheels of Jim's car. It looked like some monster whose back had been broken. It was a large Peckwith-Pierce touring car, and the force of the crash had twisted and smashed the huge chassis. Several men were gathered around the car, examining it with the aid of a barn-lantern.

"Where were the bodies found?" I asked, my voice trembling.

"Mrs. Felderson was over there on the bank. She was thrown out likely when the car left the road. Mr. Felderson's body was under the machine."

While the thought of the heavy weight crushing the life out of Jim sickened me, I thanked God that death must have been instantaneous.

"Do you know who found them, Sergeant?"

He pointed to a man standing by the wreck. "That man over there. He found them and took them to the hospital after sending one of his friends to notify the police."

The man evidently heard our voices, and came over to us.

"Is this the inspector?" he asked.

"No," I replied, "I am Mr. Felderson's brother-in-law."

"Oh, I'm sorry!" he said quickly. "May I express my deep, deep sympathy?"

"Thank you. Will you tell me how you discovered the accident?"

"I had been out to Blandesville on business and was returning with a party of friends. As we neared the bridge, one of them caught sight of the upturned automobile in the creek, and we stopped. We found Mrs. Felderson first, being attracted by her moans. We went at once to the car, and as there were four of us, we were able to lift the automobile sufficiently to get Mr. Felderson from under it. We knew that the woman was still living, but none of us was doctor enough to tell whether Mr. Felderson was alive or not. We carried them quickly to our car and hurried to St. Mary's, dropping one of my friends at the North District Station to inform the police what had occurred. Afterward we drove back here, thinking we might be wanted in case there was an investigation."

"Did you see the lights of any car ahead of you, as you came along the road?" I asked. "Did any car pass you, going in the same direction?"

"A car turned in ahead of us from the Millerstown Road about ten minutes before."

"Do you think that might have been the car that was partly responsible for this accident?" I queried.

"Of course, no one could be sure in a situation of that kind, but I wouldn't doubt it at all. It left us behind as if we were tied."

Another car had driven up while we were talking and our policeman had gone over to it at once. He came back now, accompanied by a short heavy-set man in plain clothes.

"I am Inspector Robinson, detailed to examine into this affair. Were you the man who discovered the accident?" he asked, addressing my companion.

"Yes, Inspector; Pickering is my name. I'm with the Benefit Insurance Company."

He told the circumstances of the discovery to the plain-clothes man, who, all the time Pickering was talking, bustled up and down and around the car. Finally he made Pickering show him just where the bodies lay.

"Distressing, distressing," the inspector chirped, "dreadful accident, dreadful indeed, but quite to be expected with fast driving. If they will risk their lives——"

"Inspector," I broke in, "I am the brother-in-law of the man who drove that car. While he was a fast driver, he was not a careless one. I've never known him to have an accident before." The little man irritated me.

"That's the way it always happens," he came back at me; "they take risks a dozen times and get away with them, and then—Blooey!!"

"But aren't you going to find the other car?" I demanded.

"What other car?" he snapped.

"The one that must have been coming from the opposite direction; that caused this accident."

"Do you know there was any such car?" he bristled.

"There must have been," I answered. "No accident has ever happened here except under such circumstances. Besides, Mr. Pickering saw a car turn into this road ahead of him not ten minutes before the accident."

Robinson looked from me to Pickering as though we were both conspiring to defeat justice.

"Did you see such a car?" he barked at Pickering.

"A car turned out of the Millerstown Road and went toward the city about ten minutes before we discovered the bodies," Pickering replied evenly.

"Why didn't you say so?" the detective asked sharply. "What kind of a car was it?"

"A black limousine with wire wheels. I couldn't see the number."

Robinson's humor seemed to have come back.

"Now we're getting on," he said, rubbing his hands. "That's better. That's much better. If you gentlemen had just told me that in the first place we'd have saved all this time."

He turned to the motorcycle policeman. "Feeney, go over to Millerstown and inquire if a black limousine with wire wheels stopped there to-night between eight and nine o'clock."

A figure, unnoticed in the darkness, approached. It proved to be a lanky farmer, who spoke with a decided drawl.

"I reckon I kin help ye thar. They was a big limozine tourin' car with wire wheels went through Millerstown 'bout ha'f past eight, quat' t' nine. I know, 'cause it durn near run me down."

"Do you live in Millerstown?" the inspector questioned.

"Yep! Come over t' see the accident."

"Did that auto stop in Millerstown?"

The farmer chuckled and expectorated. "It didn't even hesitate."

"Can you tell us anything else about it?" I spoke up.

The inspector glared at me. "I'll conduct this investigation, Mr.—err——"

The farmer scratched his head. "Waal, nothin' much. It went too blamed fast fer me to git mor'n a right good look, but I did gee that it was full o' men an' the tail-light was bu'sted an' they wa'n't no license on it."

"You're sure of that?" the inspector asked.

"Yep!" he said, "I'm sure, 'cause I was goin' to report 'em."

Again the inspector turned to Feeney, who had been listening intently.

"Feeney, go in and tell the chief to issue instructions to all the force to keep an eye out for a black limousine with wire wheels, a broken tail-light and no license tag! My friend," he said, turning to the farmer, "I thank you for your information. By to-morrow night we'll have that car and the parties concerned. By gad! They had their nerve, running away after the accident. The damned rascals—killing people and then running away. I'll grill their toes for them."

The malice of the little detective, his readiness to jump from one conclusion to another, reminded me for all the world of some disagreeable, little, barking dog that chases every passing vehicle.

I bade him good night, shook hands with Pickering and was on my way back to my car, when another automobile drove up. Three men jumped out, and as they passed in front of the lamps, I recognized Lawrence Brown and Fred Paisley, from the club; the third man was Frank Woods. As I caught sight of his well-set-up figure, all the hatred I had for him seemed to rise in my throat and choke me. Try as I would I couldn't separate him from the tragedy. When the farmer said the black limousine was full of men, I realized that Frank Woods couldn't have been one of them, and yet, so great was my distrust of the man, that I felt like accusing him on the spot.

Larry Brown caught sight of me and wrung my hand. "Dammit, old man, I can't fell you how sorry I am." Paisley patted me on the back. "If there is anything we can do, Thompson——"

I shook my head and tears came to my eyes. They made me realize poignantly how much I had lost. Woods didn't join us. He knew if he tried to sympathize with me, after the affair the other day, that I would throttle him for his hypocrisy.

"Was Jim killed outright?" Brown asked.

"Yes! And there's one chance in a thousand for Helen."

Both men started. "Was Mrs. Felderson there? They telephoned us at the club that Jim had been killed, but we didn't know she was with him."

They glanced at each other and then at Woods, who was standing by the side of the overturned car.

"You'd better tell him, Larry," Paisley muttered.

"Doesn't he know?" I asked.

"Of course not," replied Brown. "He was out there at the club with us. I'm afraid it will hit him awfully hard."

He stepped over to Woods and, taking him by the arm, they disappeared into the darkness.

We heard a choking cry, and the next moment Woods came running toward us. His face was distorted with horror and his eyes were almost starting from his head.

"Thompson, for God's sake, tell me he lies! Tell me he lies!" he shrieked. "Helen wasn't in that car?"

The old suspicions came tumbling back an hundredfold and I turned cold all over.

"It is true," I said, "Mrs. Felderson is in the hospital at the point of death."

With a stifled groan, Woods sank to the ground and buried his face in his shaking hands.

6

A Clue and a Verdict

I drove home with my thoughts in a tumult. The look on Woods' face and the vehemence of his words made me sure he was in some way responsible for Jim's death. I walked the floor for hours trying to build up my case against him. He had sworn to kill Jim, unless he let Helen go, and he must have known that afternoon that not only was Jim going to keep Helen from him, but that he had the proof with which to ruin him forever. He had planned to have it out with Jim at the country-club, knowing it would be a cold damp night and that few people would be out there. He had emphatically stated that Jim should come alone and should be there promptly at half-past eight. All those facts pointed to the man's guilt and I felt sure that in some way I should be able to unearth the proof.

I knew I ought to sleep, but sleep was the last thing I could do. Twice I called up the hospital to inquire after Helen, but they could tell me nothing. Had the operation been successful? Yes, she had come through it. Would she get well? Ah, that they could not say. They would let me know if there was any change. I sent a telegram to Jim's uncle in the West, the only relative Jim ever corresponded with, and told him to notify any others to whom the news would be of vital interest.

Toward five o'clock, when dawn was just graying the windows, I threw myself on my bed. I suddenly realized I was extremely tired, yet my brain was buzzing like a dynamo. Pictures and scenes from the last few days flashed through my mind: the vindictive look in Helen's eyes after the fight with Woods; that table being wheeled out of Helen's room at the hospital, with the moaning white bundle on it; the upturned car pricked out of the darkness by the automobile lamps, and finally, Frank Woods' face when he heard that Helen had been in the car. With the realization that I ought to get up and close the window, where the morning breeze was idly flapping the curtain, I fell asleep.

I awoke with a start, to find the room flooded with golden sunlight. A glance at the clock on the mantel-shelf showed that it was after nine. My body was cramped and stiff and I felt stale and musty from having slept in my clothes. It was only after a cold shower and a complete change that I felt refreshed enough to pick up the threads where I had dropped them the night before.

Again, like the sudden aching of a tooth, came the heart-breaking realization that Jim was dead. With it came also anxiety for Helen's condition, so I called up the hospital at once. They could only say she had not recovered consciousness, but seemed to be resting comfortably.

I went down to the office to tell the stenographers they might have a vacation until after the funeral, and to lock up. The first person I found there was Inspector Robinson, who was calmly reading over the correspondence on Jim's desk. With all the "sang-froid" in the world, he met my infuriated gaze.

"Good morning, Mr. Thompson. Thought there might be something here touching on the case." He waved a hand toward Jim's letter basket.

"Have you found the black limousine?" I asked.

"Certainly, my dear man, certainly! We've not only found the car, but we found the people who were in the car and they know nothing about the accident. My first explanation was the right one, as I knew it would be. Felderson was driving recklessly, saw the bridge, put on the brakes, skidded—was killed."

"But why should he put on his brakes at the bridge?" I queried.

"I've thought of that," he smiled. "Perfectly logical. There's a nasty bump at the bridge and he naturally didn't want to jar Mrs. Felderson."

"So he turned into the ditch and pitched her out on her head instead," I jeered. "That's all poppy-cock. I've taken that bridge at full speed a hundred times without a jar."

"It's immaterial anyway," he snapped, frowning at me. "You can't make any fool mystery out of it. The point is that Mr. Felderson put on his brakes rapidly, perhaps for a dog or a rabbit, and skidded into the ditch."

"It's not immaterial!" I burst out angrily. "There was a real reason for his putting his brakes on rapidly. He was afraid of hitting something, or being hit himself. Who was the driver of that other car?"

"The son of one of the biggest men in the state, Karl Schreiber."

"Karl Schreiber?" I cried. "The son of the German Socialist, who was put in jail for dodging the draft?" I grabbed him by the arm. "Quick, man! Who were the others with him?"

Robinson gazed at me with a stupid frown.

"Two reporters from *The Sun*, a fellow by the name of Pederson, Otto Metzger and that Russian, Zalnitch, who just got out of prison."

"Zalnitch!" I yelled exultantly.

Zalnitch! The man Jim had sent to prison and who had threatened revenge. Metzger, who had been his accomplice all along. Schreiber, who hated Jim and all the virile Americanism that he stood for. Pederson and the two reporters I didn't know, but they were no doubt of the same vile breed. A fine gang of cutthroats who would have liked nothing better than to get rid of Jim. They probably saw his big search-light, that makes his car easily recognizable, and realized their opportunity had come. They had driven toward him as though to smash into him and made Jim take the ditch to get out of the way. That explained the sudden jamming on of his brakes that had caused him to skid and overturn. All these thoughts passed through my mind as I heard the names of the men in the black limousine.

"Inspector," I said, "I am fully convinced that the men in the black limousine are responsible for my brother-in-law's accident."

"What makes you think that?" he demanded, eying me narrowly.

"Because all of them had reason to hate and fear my brother-in-law. Zalnitch, since his release, has sworn he would get even with Mr. Felderson for putting him in prison.

Metzger felt the same way. As for Schreiber, I'm sure if he could have manipulated that car so as to cause an accident to Mr. Felderson, he would have done it."

"You're crazy," Robinson sneered. "This thing's gone to your head.

How could they have known it was your brother-in-law's car?"

"By the big search-light in front. It's the only car in the state with such a search-light. Mr. Felderson's car was so fast that the police sometimes used it, and he had their permission to wear that light, as you probably know. Also, it may have been dark enough to use the search-light and yet light enough so that a car could be distinguished at a hundred feet. If there was any light at all, that big Peckwith-Pierce car could be recognized by any one." He was impressed. I could see it by the thoughtful, shrewd look that, came into his eyes. Already, he was making arrests by the wholesale, in his mind.

"But I can't go pulling these men for murder on such slight evidence as that," he exploded.

"No one wants you to," I said sharply. "All I want you to do is to help me find out whether those men were present when the accident happened."

The idea of helping me didn't please him at all. As soon as I had spoken I saw my error in not putting it the other way around.

"Now, Mr. Thompson, you better keep out of this," he advised, getting to his feet. "I know that you are anxious to find out if these men had anything to do with Mr. Felderson's death, but the case is in good hands. We professionals can do a lot better, when there's no amateurs messing about. You leave it to me!"

"Just as you say," I acquiesced. "Get busy, though, and if you find out anything, let me know!"

Robinson stood a minute, turning his derby hat in his hands. I knew what he was after.

"By the way," I added. "I'll pay all expenses."

His face brightened at once. "Well, now, that's good of you, Mr. Thompson. I wasn't going to suggest anything like that, but it'll help a lot."

I handed over several bills, which he pocketed with satisfaction.

"Don't you worry a minute, Mr. Thompson. We'll get those birds yet. I was pretty sure they had something to do with it, all the time. You've got the best man in the department on the job."

He put on his derby hat with a flourish and trotted out the door. I recalled that I had told Mary I would see her, so I dismissed the stenographers and locked up the office. It was a perfect morning, with all the warm spicy perfumes of Indian summer. Overhead, a blue sky was filled with tumbled clouds of snowy whiteness. The rain of the night before was still on the grass and the trees, giving a dewy fragrance to the air that was invigorating.

Now that I had found a possible solution to the tragedy, I was filled with enthusiasm. I felt that if I could bring Jim's murderers to trial, I would conduct such a case for the prosecution as would send them up for life. They had succeeded in carrying out their threats, but I would make them pay for it.

I stopped in front of Mary's house and honked the horn. She opened the door and came quickly to the car. The tragic news of the night before had taken the laughter out of her eyes and the buoyancy from her step.

"I could cry my eyes out, Bupps," she said as she climbed into the car.

"Don't do it, or I'll start, too," I responded, a lump coming in my throat.

"How did it happen?" she asked, as we drove away. "The papers gave a long account, but said it was an accident."

"Zalnitch did it, Mary. At least, I'm almost sure it was he." I told her what I had learned during the morning, and as I talked, I finally touched on Frank Woods' strange words of the night before.

"You don't think he had anything to do with it, do you, Bupps?"

"No," I said. "I did think so, but I have changed my mind since this morning. I suppose it was just his grief that made him act so queerly."

"He does love Helen, Bupps," Mary murmured. "Helen got quite confidential while she was staying with me, and the things she told me about Woods made me see he was really in love with her."

"Yes, I suppose he does love her," I responded, "but he had no right to take her away from Jim."

"It's the man who takes a woman, whether he has the right or not, that wins," responded Mary seriously.

I looked at her and wondered whether she was growing the least bit personal. She was looking straight ahead, with an unsmiling gaze. As I glanced at her, there beside me, with the breeze blowing wisps of golden hair around her temples, I got panic-stricken.

"Mary—" I began.

"Watch where you are going, Bupps!"

I fastened my eyes on the street ahead, but only for an instant. With Jim gone, I was going to be fearfully lonesome. I glanced at her again.

"Mary, I know this isn't the right time or place, but—"

"Let's go to the hospital and find out about Helen," she interposed quickly. She knew we were going there all the time. The mention of Helen brought me back to earth with a snap, and made me realize I had no business talking about love at such a time. Yet never in my life did I feel more like telling Mary how much I wanted her.

We had no sooner entered the cool hall of St. Mary's than the little intern with glasses, whom I had seen the night before, came hurrying up to me.

"Mr. Thompson, we have been telephoning every place for you."

My heart jumped to my throat. "Is Mrs. Felderson—?"

"No," he responded, "Mrs. Felderson is still unconscious. It is Mr. Felderson. The coroner has made an important discovery."

I waved for Mary to stay where she was and hurried down-stairs, where Jim's body lay. It had not been moved before the coroner's inquest. The room was dark and several people were gathered around the inquest table. All eyes were turned on me as I entered the room. A portly man detached himself from the group and came toward me.

"Mr. Thompson?"

"Yes."

"I am the coroner. In making my inquest, I find that death was not due to the automobile smash-up. Mr. Felderson was shot through the head, from behind. We have rendered a verdict of murder."

7

I Turn Detective

Murdered! For a moment I was stupefied by the doctor's revelation, and then, as he went on to describe the course of the bullet, and certain technical aspects of the case, a sudden rush of thankfulness came over me. Let me explain! The coroner had given a verdict of murder by person or persons unknown. From the first moment I heard of the accident I was certain there was something sinister about it, but had little on which to base my belief. The coroner's verdict substantiated my suspicions and gave me a chance to work in the open; to bring into court, if possible, the people I suspected.

Murder by person or persons unknown? I knew the persons: Zalnitch, Metzger, Schreiber. They must have recognized the car as it came toward them and taken a shot as they went by. My thoughts were recalled from their wanderings by an unexpected sentence of the coroner's. I had been following him vaguely, but now my attention was riveted.

"One could not be sure, because of the varied course that bullets take through the body, but the shot seems to have been fired from above and behind. Unless it were otherwise proved, I'd strongly suspect that the murderer had fired the shot from the back seat of the car."

"Of course that is impossible," I said, "because in that case the murderer would have been in the accident."

"I had the same idea," he said slowly, giving me a searching look. Helen!

I felt suddenly sick and faint. I wanted air, sunlight; to get away from that darkened room and those piercing eyes that seemed to read my thoughts. I thanked him for letting me know what he had discovered, and hurriedly excused myself.

Helen! The blood pounded through my temples.

God! No!

Wilful, spoiled woman, if you will, ready to leave her husband without thought of the consequences, to go with another man; but his premeditated murderer? A thousand times, no!

I felt that with the unworthy suspicion in my mind, I could not face Mary, and I waited a moment at the bottom of the stairs before going up to meet her. There were two questions that had to be answered. Was Helen in the back seat when the car left Mary's the evening before; and had Jim told Helen about the proofs he had of Woods' irregularities? Mary was probably there when Helen and Jim left, and could answer both questions.

I wiped the perspiration from my forehead and assuming as calm an air as possible, went up-stairs. Mary was chatting with the little intern, but as soon as she saw my face, she hurried toward me.

"You look as though you'd seen a ghost. What was it, Bupps?"

"Not here!" I cautioned. "Wait until we get outside!"

We walked down the broad sunlit steps and climbed into the car. I felt like a traitor to let Mary even think that I suspected Helen, but my questions had to be answered.

"Will you have luncheon with me, Mary?"

"Certainly," she answered. "Let's go to Luigi's. We can talk quietly there."

I headed for down-town and kept my eyes on the road, dreading to put my questions into words.

"What was it, Bupps?" Mary asked.

I decided to ask what I had to ask before telling her the coroner's verdict.

"Did you see Helen leave the house with Jim yesterday?"

"Yes. I was looking out the window when they started. Why?"

I could hardly force myself to go on.

"Was Helen—did Helen get into the front seat with Jim?" I faltered.

"No. She climbed into the back," Mary replied. "They had some sort of an argument before they left. I knew Jim was excited and that Helen was angry. Of course I didn't hear all that passed between them, I tried not to hear any, but they talked very loud and were right in the next room."

"What did you hear?" I asked, my heart sinking.

"Once Jim laughed, a hard sort of laugh, and I heard Helen say, 'You lie! You know you are lying! He will disprove everything you say!' Another time I heard Helen exclaim, 'Give me that pistol! You shan't threaten him while I'm there!' I knew, of course, they were speaking of Frank Woods, but I didn't know what it was all about. But why do you ask all this, Bupps?"

"Mary," I said, and I couldn't look at her, "the coroner has given a verdict of murder."

"Murder?" Mary gasped. I nodded.

"Jim was shot from behind, while he was driving Helen out to the country-club to meet Woods, and Helen was in the back seat."

"She didn't do it!" Mary burst out. "She couldn't have done it."

"Of course she didn't do it!" I exploded. We were glaring at each other as though each was defending Helen from the other's accusation. "We know she didn't do it, but there are many who won't take our word for it. I could see by the way the coroner looked at me this morning that he is ready to accuse her of murdering Jim, and it's up to us to save her, by finding out who really is guilty."

We drove up in front of Luigi's, and I was able to get a small table, in the corner by ourselves. Although no one could have overheard us, I sat as near Mary as I could and we talked with our heads close together.

Mrs. Webster Pratt came in the door just then, with a luncheon party, and, noticing how we were engrossed, came bouncing over to the table at once.

"Poor Mr. Thompson, my heart bleeds for you—simply bleeds for you."

I got to my feet and permitted her to squeeze my hand. She squeezes your hand or pats you at the least opportunity, and this one was unequaled.

"Poor, dear Mr. Felderson. It is such a loss. I was shocked to death when I heard it. And Mrs. Felderson, the poor child, is she going to—ah—t-t-t. I was afraid so when I read it in the paper. I'm surprised to find you here. How is your poor dear mother?"

I knew that the woman would gossip all over the place about my heartlessness, unless I explained my presence in a public café so soon after Jim's death and my sister's injury.

"My mother doesn't know about it yet," I said quietly. "I didn't think her strong enough to stand the shock. I shouldn't have come here, but I had a very important matter to talk over with Miss Pendleton."

"I could see that from the way you were sitting," she giggled. "I'm afraid that you're going to give Eastbrook something to talk about as soon as this distressing thing is over." She patted my arm, beamed at Mary and swished over to her party.

"We shouldn't have come here, Mary," I said with a sour grimace.

"I forgot that old cat sometimes comes here. She'll spread it all over town that you were down here making love to me before Jim was decently buried. She'll probably say we're engaged."

"Well, I wish we were." I know I must have shown my longing in my eyes.

"Don't, please, Warren!" Mary whispered, putting her hand on my arm. "We've got too much to do. That Pratt woman drove everything out of my mind for a moment. I wish she hadn't seen us here."

I didn't feel as though I could eat a thing and neither did Mary, so I told the waiter to bring us a light salad, and sent him away.

"Mary," I said, after he had gone, "we know Helen didn't do this thing, but if you are called by the grand jury to tell what you just told me, they will bring an indictment against her in a minute."

"They couldn't!" Mary expostulated. "They couldn't believe such a thing."

"Don't you think Mrs. Webster Pratt would believe it, if she knew everything that we know?" I argued. "She'd believe it with only half as much proof, and she has just about the mental equipment of the average juryman. There'll be about four Mrs. Webster Pratts on that jury."

"What can we do, Bupps?" Mary begged with tears in her eyes.

"Well," I said, "you've got to see Helen as soon as they will let you and as often as they'll let you, so that the first time she speaks, you'll be there to hear what she says."

"But suppose she dies, Bupps?"

"Even while she is unconscious," I went on, disregarding her query, "she may say something that will give us a clue. I'm going out to the bridge right after lunch."

"What for?" Mary asked.

"To see if I can find Jim's revolver. If it had been found on Helen, the coroner would have told me this morning, I think. Of course, they may not have taken it at all. In that case it will still be at your house. If Helen took it with her, it must have fallen out when the car turned over, and if it did, I must get it before anybody else does."

The waiter interrupted here with the salad. Mary dabbled with hers a bit and then said:

"Bupps, hadn't I better get out of town?"

"No," I replied. "They'd be sure to find you, and when you gave your testimony, it would hurt Helen just that much more."

"But I can't stand up before them and tell what I heard. I'll lie first." Her lovely little face clouded up as though she were going to cry.

"You'll do nothing of the kind!" I insisted. "We know Helen didn't do it. Don't we?"

"Ye-es." Her tone was not convincing.

"Well, then, whatever we say can't hurt her. And we're bound to find out who the guilty persons are."

"But, Bupps, who could it have been?" she asked anxiously.

"I still think it was Zalnitch and the men who were with him, but it might have been Woods. I'm going to find out everything he did last night. It may throw some light on the case. After all, he is the one who had the most to gain by Jim's death, and his words of last night were mighty queer."

I paid the waiter and we left the café. On the way to Mary's I stopped at the undertaker's and made arrangements for Jim's burial. The man in charge was the saddest looking person I have ever seen. He had a woebegone look about him that was infectious—made you want to weep for him or with him. He discussed the funeral arrangements in a hushed voice and finished by whispering, "I sincerely hope what the papers are hinting is not so."

"What's that?" I asked.

"The noon edition of *The Sun* says, 'The finger of suspicion points very strongly to Mrs. Felderson.'"

I hurried out to the car and jumped in.

"Mary, we've got to work fast."

"Is Helen suspected?" she asked.

"Yes. *The Sun* is more than hinting."

The news seemed to bring out the fight in Mary.

"Well, we'll prove her innocent."

When we reached the Pendletons' we hurried into the house and went at once to the room where Jim and Helen had their argument. The revolver was not there.

8

It Looks Bad for Helen

I drove Mary to the hospital with my spirits at lowest ebb. If *The Sun* were going to try to convict Helen of the murder, I realized that we had a hard fight ahead of us, for that yellow sheet was most zealous in hounding down any one who happened to be socially prominent, and in demanding punishment. The blacker the scandal, the deeper they dug, and the more details they gave to their gluttonous, filth-loving public. They would be particularly eager here, for they had no love for Jim, due to the stand he took against them during the war.

I knew the reporters would be hot on my trail and that sooner or later they would interview Mary. So I determined that Mary should spend as much time as possible at the hospital, feeling sure the reporters would not be allowed in the room where Helen lay, battered and unconscious. As for me, I wanted to get to the bridge on the Blandesville Road as quickly as possible and from there to the country-club to inquire what Woods had done the night before. I made up my mind I'd lead the reporters a merry old chase before they ran me to earth, and when they did, I'd tell them nothing. I also wanted to get in touch with Robinson as soon as I could, to find out whether he had discovered anything new of Zalnitch and his confederates—but that could wait until evening.

At the hospital they were at first opposed to having any one in the room with Helen, who still lay in a coma, but with the help of one of the nurses in charge, it was at last arranged.

As I drove over the road to the club, the bleak barrenness of the country struck me anew. Twenty-four hours before Jim had been alive. Twenty-four hours before we had been in our office discussing the proof of Woods' guilt, and Woods had telephoned to Jim, asking him to come to the country-club alone. My suspicions of the man stirred afresh, so that when I came to the bridge and found no one there, I decided to leave my search for the revolver until later and go straight on to the club.

It was still early for the golfers and the bridge players and there were only a few people there. These, of course, came up to me and pressed my hand with genuine sympathy. I realized how many, many friends Jim had and what a loss his death was to them all.

As soon as I could disengage myself I hunted up Jackson, the negro head-waiter and general house-man, who knows everything that happens at the club. He had just finished his dinner and I drew him into the cloak-room so that our talk might be uninterrupted. I took out a five dollar bill and held it up before his expectant eyes.

"Do you see that, Jackson?" I questioned.

"Yas, indeed Ah sees it, suh! Ah may be gittin' old but Ah ain't blind yit. Ah'll giv you whut you wants, instan'ly."

He started to leave, but I grabbed him.

"That's not what I want, Jackson," I laughed. Since the prohibition law went into effect, it has been only through some such ritual that "wets" can get theirs at the club. "All I want is to ask you a few questions."

"Fo' dat money?" His teeth gleamed. I nodded.

"Mr. Woods was here last night?" I asked, abruptly.

"Yas, suh."

"What time did he come in?"

"Ah cain't raghtly say, Mist' Thompsin, but he had dinnah out heah 'bout seben-thuty," he answered.

"Did he leave the club after that?"

"Not 'til de telephone call come whut says Mist' Feldahson ben killt. Den he lef wif Mist' Brown an' Mist' Paisley."

"You're sure he was here all that time?" I asked.

"No, sah, I ain't suah, but Ah seen him ev'y now an' den thu de ev'nin'.'"

"Was he here at quarter past eight?" I questioned.

"He was heah at twenty-fahv minutes past eight, Ah knows, cause Ah done brought him a drink."

"You're sure of that?"

"Yas, suh! Positive!" the negro answered. "'Cause Ah looked at de clock raght den an' der."

As near as I could figure, the accident had happened about eight-ten or eight-fifteen and the bridge was six miles away from the club. Woods couldn't have been at the bridge at the time of the tragedy and got back to the club by eighty twenty-five. Still, he might have had an accomplice.

"Thank you, Jackson," I said, giving him the money. "Just forget that I asked you any questions!"

The darky chuckled. "Ah done fohgot 'em befoh you evah asted 'em, suh. Thank you, suh!"

As I passed into the big, central living-room, Paisley came in.

"What was this I saw in *The Sun*?" he asked.

"The sort of rot that nasty sheet always prints," I said.

"Nothing to it of course. I thought not. You don't feel like golfing?"

I shook my head. "Not to-day, old chap. By the way, were you with Frank Woods when the news of Jim's death reached the club?"

"Yes—why?" he asked.

"You won't think it too strange if I ask you how he appeared to take it?" I said, trying to make my remark seem as casual as possible. Seeing the puzzled expression on his face, I added: "I know it is a peculiar thing to ask, but please don't think any more about it than you can help, and just answer."

"Why—" Paisley began, a little flustered, "why he took it just the way the rest of us took it, I suppose. I don't remember exactly."

"Did he seem surprised?" I questioned.

"Of course," Paisley answered, "He didn't seem relieved?"

"Say, what the devil are you driving at, Thompson?" Paisley burst out.

I saw I could get nothing from him so I left him looking after me with a perplexed and somewhat indignant gaze. As a detective it seemed I might make a good plumber. I knew very well he would not repeat my questions, but it would be just like good old Paisley to worry himself to death trying to solve them.

I drove back to the bridge, determined to find the revolver, if possible, and then hunt up Inspector Robinson to learn what he had to report. Apparently, my suspicions of Frank Woods were groundless. He had had dinner at the club and then waited around for Jim to keep his appointment. He had been seen by Jackson at eight twenty-five; Jackson was positive of that fact. Ten or fifteen minutes at the most in which to go six miles to the bridge and back to the club, put up his car and ask Jackson for a drink. The thing couldn't be done. He had heard of Jim's death with surprise and had heard of Helen's injury with the greatest horror. There seemed to be no doubt of one thing: no matter how much he wished for Jim's death, no matter how much he benefited by the murder, Frank Woods, himself, didn't do the killing.

An automobile was standing at the bridge when I got there and I cursed the whim that had sent me to the club on a false scent and kept me from having an uninterrupted search for the weapon. When I saw, however, that the driver of the automobile was Inspector Robinson, I was greatly relieved, for this would not only give me a chance to learn what he had discovered concerning the men in the black limousine, but would not interfere with the search for Jim's gun. Robinson had his coat off and his sleeves rolled up and was fishing around the edge of the little creek with his hands. So engrossed was he in his task that I was almost upon him before he looked up.

"Good afternoon, Inspector," I addressed him. "What are you doing, digging for gold or making mud pies?"

"I'm gettin' bait to catch a sucker," he snarled. "You must have thought you had one this morning."

"What do you mean?" I asked.

"All that bunk you handed me about Schreiber and the men in the black limousine. That was a fine stall you pulled. I might have known you was tryin' to cover up somebody's tracks."

He dried his hands on a rather flamboyant, yellow handkerchief.

"I haven't the least idea what you are talking about," I replied coldly.

"Oh, you haven't, haven't you?" the little man burst out malignantly. "You're innocent, you are! Too damned innocent! I suppose you didn't know that your brother-in-law was shot in the back of the head and that your sister was the only one that was with him when it was done. I suppose that's news—eh?"

My heart stood still as I heard his words. So he was after the proof that Helen did it. He had read the insinuations in *The Sun* and had abandoned his work against Schreiber and Zalnitch for the fresher trail.

"I found out this morning that my brother-in-law was shot, but that only makes the case look the blacker for those who openly threatened his life."

"Among whom was your beautiful sister," the detective retorted acidly.

"How do you know that?" I demanded.

"From her maid and all the rest of the servants in the house. I found that out when I went up to take another squint at the automobile. You thought you were pretty smart sendin' me on a wild-goose chase after a couple of cracked Socialists, when all the time you knew it was your own sister done the thing. Tried to keep me off the track by slippin' me a little dough. Well, it didn't work, see? There's your dough back." He threw a crumpled wad of bills on the ground at my feet. "No one saw you give it to me, but I ain't takin' any chances, you may have marked those bills. From now on I work alone without any theories from you."

"Look here, Inspector!" I demanded, "I was in earnest when I told you I wanted you to find out all you could about the men in the black limousine. I'm sure they had something to do with Mr. Felderson's death. I didn't try to bribe you, nor throw you off the right track. Even though my sister did have a little unpleasantness with her husband, it was no serious difference."

I determined to find out just how much Robinson knew.

"She was utterly incapable of doing an act like this. What possible motive could she have?"

I could see that Robinson was rather impatiently waiting for me to go before continuing his search.

"Well, I ain't found out her motive yet. That can wait. It might have been money or jealousy."

"Money?" I scoffed. "My sister had plenty; more than she could use. And as for her being jealous of her husband, that is even more ridiculous."

The little man eyed me angrily. "I said that the motive could wait. There's no tellin' what a society woman will do. She may have been crazy for all I know. But I ain't, and all your arguin' is just so much time wasted. You think those guys in the automobile done it. I don't. I think your sister done it. You don't. All right, then, you take your road and I'll take mine, and we'll see who comes out ahead."

He turned and started back to where he had been hunting when I came up.

"May I ask what you expect to find here?" I queried, walking after him.

"Sure you can ask," he replied. As he found me following, he turned and snapped: "Say, what the hell are you hangin' around here for, anyway?"

"I merely wanted to ask what you had discovered about the men in the black limousine.

That's why I stopped."

"Well, you've found out, haven't you? *Nothin'*. All right then, you go on into the city and see if you can find out anything more!"

I walked on down the sloping bank, searching the ground to see if I could find the gun that might reveal so much. I could feel the eyes of the inspector boring into my back.

"What are you looking for?" he demanded.

"A cuff-link," I answered easily. "I think I lost one here last night. You didn't happen to find it, did you?"

"A cuff-link? Humph!" he grunted. "No, I haven't found it, but I wouldn't be surprised if I was lookin' for that same cuff-link."

All this time I was searching the bank with my eyes. A scrubby, little bush overhung the creek and I kicked at it with my foot. There was a "plopp" as though something heavy had dropped into the water. Instinctively I knew it was the object for which we were both searching, and I turned to find the inspector eying me quizzically.

"What was that noise?"

"What noise?" I asked.

"Sounded as though that precious cuff-link of yours had dropped into the water." He started for me, and as he did so, I bent down quickly and plunged my arm into the water. My fingers closed on the revolver just as he came bounding toward me. With a quick shove I pushed it far into the soft clay of the bank, and, grabbing a rock off the bottom of the creek, withdrew my arm from the water and slipped the rock into my pocket. The red-faced little detective was peering over my shoulder as I turned. Rarely have I seen a man so angry.

"Give me what you pulled out of that creek!" he almost screamed.

"What for, Inspector?" I asked quietly.

"Never mind what for. You give me what you found in that creek, or I'll—" he grabbed me by the shoulder.

"All right," I said; "all right, Inspector, don't get so excited over nothing. It's yours." I pulled the muddy rock from my coat pocket and gravely handed it to him. "It was only an ordinary, every-day rock. I didn't know you were a geologist."

He pounced on me and ran his fingers over my person. Red-faced, he surveyed me.

"I ain't a geologist, but I am a criminologist, and just one more of your monkey tricks like that and I'll put you where you'll have time to study a lot of rocks and do a lot of thinkin' before bein' funny again. Now, you get out! Get into that car as quick as you can, if you know what's good for you!"

Hoping I could retrieve the revolver later, and realizing that nothing could be gained by staying there longer, I started toward the car. I had hardly taken five steps when I heard a joyful yell and turned to see Robinson struggling to his feet, the muddy revolver in his hand.

"Here's your cuff-link," he cried. "Before I'm through you'll find that this ain't a cuff-link, but a necklace for the neck of that pretty sister of yours. You, with your Socialists and your cuff-buttons, tryin' to keep me from gettin' what I go after. Well, it didn't work! It don't usually, when I go after somethin'. It didn't work, did it?"

"No. It didn't work," I admitted.

"Oh, I don't blame you," Robinson went on, mollified by his success and the soft tone of my reply; "I'd of done the same thing in your place, if my sister was a murderer."

The word "murderer" acted like an electric shock on me.

"She didn't do it, I tell you; she couldn't have done it!"

"Now, Mr. Thompson," Robinson began in a soothing voice. "These things happen in even the best families sometimes. You mustn't take it too hard."

"Will you let me examine that revolver?" I demanded.

"Why, no. I can't let you examine it. But I'll examine it when I get ready."

"Will you be so good as to do it now?" I asked.

"What for?"

"Because it may not have been fired at all. That would make things look entirely different, you know."

The inspector took out the gaudy handkerchief again and wiped the mud off the barrel and the grip. I had shoved the pistol barrel foremost into the bank so the muzzle was filled with clay. It was Jim's—a "32" automatic.

"It won't be spoilin' any evidence by my cleanin' this mud off the outside, because you put that there yourself," the detective said, wiping the pistol carefully. He released the spring and pulled out the clip. I saw a cartridge at the top of the clip and exclaimed:

"There! You see? That gun was never fired!"

The inspector looked at me with a pitying smile.

"Now, that's where you're wrong, Mr. Thompson. You see, you don't know the inner workings of an automatic. When a gun like this is fired, it discharges the old shell and a new cartridge comes to the top of the clip. There are only three cartridges left in this clip."

"Do you mean to say that my sister fired more than one shot?" I asked sarcastically.

"Not at all, not at all," the little man responded airily. "There were probably only four cartridges in the gun in the first place. You're gettin' all excited over this thing. Of course, I don't blame you, Mr. Thompson, for tryin' to fight against facts, but it certainly looks bad for sister."

I got into my car and started home, my heart dead within me. It certainly did look bad for Helen.

9

Look Out, Jim

A good general realizes when he is beaten and changes his tactics accordingly. Where I had been certain of Zalnitch's guilt before, and had planned his prosecution, now, with the sickening certainty that it was my sister herself who was guilty, I began to plan her defense. Yes, I'll admit right now, the gun convinced me. I had been certain that Jim had not been killed through careless driving, that is why I had been so insistent that Inspector Robinson should hunt down those responsible for his death. Now that it was too late, I cursed myself for not having let well-enough alone and aided the coroner in giving a verdict of accidental death. My suspicions against Zalnitch had been based on the knowledge that he hated Jim and would have done anything to put him out of the way. Coincidence had brought him over the same road that Jim had traveled a few minutes before his death. This had strengthened my suspicions, but the case would have been hard to prove, while the evidence against Helen was too pronounced to be disregarded. Woods, too, had gained my suspicions, and yet he was miles away from the murder. I realized suddenly that I had been refusing to look at the obvious in order that I might place the guilt where I wanted to believe it lay. Yet it did seem the irony of fate that the two men benefiting by Jim's death should have had nothing to do with it.

Helen did it! As the awful realization of what that meant came over me, I hoped, for a brief second, that death would take her and so spare her the consequences of her act. It would be such an easy way out. I felt sure that if she died I could hush the whole thing up. *The Sun* could be bought, if enough money was offered.

These gruesome thoughts carried me into the city almost before I knew it. I stopped at the house to change my muddy clothes, before going to the hospital to get Mary, and learned from the maid that mother had been asking for me. I went quickly to her room. She was lying in bed and at first I thought she was asleep, but she turned as I approached her.

"Is that you, Warren?" she asked softly.

"Yes, mother. Stella said you wanted to see me." I bent down and kissed her lightly. She reached up and put her thin weak arms around my neck.

"Warren, is there anything wrong? If there is you must tell me."

"No, mother. What made you think that?" I asked.

She slowly withdrew her arms and let them fall at her side.

"I don't know. I seemed to feel that something had happened. Just lying here, I felt afraid for you children—and then there were so many people ringing the bell and the telephone, I was afraid that some accident had happened to you or Helen."

I patted her wan cheek. "It's just your imagination. The only thing wrong is that my dearest, little mother isn't as well and strong as her good-for-nothing son."

I kissed her again, and she smiled up at me. "I'm so glad," she whispered. "I was worried."

I almost choked when I got outside. If Helen should recover and be put on trial, it would kill mother, I felt sure. And I would be left alone in the world. Down-stairs, I asked Stella who had called, and she told me the reporters had been trying to find me all day.

During the drive to the hospital, I tried to focus my mind on Helen's defense, but all the force seemed to have been sapped out of me. I felt weak and miserable and unutterably lonely.

At the hospital, they received me with the quiet sympathy that strengthens you in spite of yourself and gives you hope. Doctor Forbes, who had operated on Helen the night before, was in the office. He had just come from Helen's room and he reported her condition to be "extremely satisfactory."

"There is only one thing that worries me," he said. "Your sister seems to have something on her mind that keeps her from resting as quietly as I could wish. It is some real or fancied danger that repeats itself over and over in her delirium. If we could only hit on something that would ease her mind of those fears, I should have every reason to believe she'd get well. I say this to you because you are her brother and are no doubt acquainted with what has happened to her in the last few weeks, and may be able to suggest what it is she fears."

"Perhaps it is the accident itself," I offered.

He shook his head. "It may be, but I think not. However, suppose you step into the room and listen to what she says. If we can only rid her of her fears and get her to rest quietly, I am positive she will recover."

I shook his hand warmly and went upstairs to Helen's room. I knew what it was Helen feared. The consequences of her crime. The terrible fear of public prosecution for the murder of her husband was torturing her poor delirious brain. For a moment I forgave her everything and pitied her from the depths of my heart.

The smell of ether lay thick in the air as I walked down the long corridor to Helen's room. I knocked softly at the door and a white-capped nurse opened it a little way, her finger to her lips. I beckoned her outside and told her Doctor Forbes wished me to find out, if I could, what troubled my sister's mind.

As we entered, I saw Mary sitting by the bed, holding the hand of the poor white figure that lay, death-like, beneath the sheet. Helen's head was swathed in bandages, except for the oval of her face. She looked quite like some fair nun who had said her last "Ava." It was impossible to believe that it was her hand that had fired the shot that killed Jim, and if she lived, that she would have to face the world a murderer.

Mary only glanced up at me for a moment and then turned her eyes again to Helen's lips to catch any sound that might pass them. As I watched her sitting there so patiently, a little pale from her cramped vigil by the bedside, a great tenderness welled up in my heart, for her. Just then Helen's lips began to move. At first the words were inaudible, although Mary leaned forward to catch them. Then with a half-cry, in which there was a perfect agony of fear——

"Look out, Jim! It's going to hit us! Oh-oh-oh——"

The voice died away and was succeeded by moans, low and trembling. Mary glanced up with a startled look in her eyes. The nurse went quickly to the bedside and soothed the impatient hand that was plucking at the sheets. As for me, my forehead was bathed in sweat and tears were running down my cheeks, but a joy throbbed and sang through my heart till I felt that I should suffocate unless I left that ether-filled room for the open air.

I tiptoed toward the door and caught a nod from Mary as I passed, which said she would join me later. For a second, after I closed the door, I couldn't move. My legs failed me and I felt I was going to faint. Gathering all my strength, I stumbled over to a chair by the window and sat down.

I think I should have dropped to my knees and thanked God right there, if I hadn't feared that my prayers would have been interrupted. That cry, "Look out, Jim!" proved not only that Helen had nothing whatever to do with Jim's death, but that she had tried to warn him of his danger. "It's going to hit us!" What could that mean but that my first theory was correct, that the men in the black limousine had recognized Jim's car and had tried to run him into the ditch? Schreiber and Zalnitch were at the bottom of it, after all, and Helen was innocent.

As I had hoped she would die, when I thought her guilty, now I hoped and prayed she would live. I recalled Doctor Forbes' words: "If we could only hit on something that would ease her mind of those fears, I would have every reason to believe she would get well." I could at least tell him the cause of the fear and leave it to him to find a remedy. With Helen well, ready to testify as to the details of that tragic night, we would certainly bring Jim's murderers to trial.

The door opened and Mary came out. I rose and walked over to her, my eyes still betraying the emotion Helen's words had roused in me.

"You heard what she said?" Mary breathed.

"We knew she didn't do it, didn't we?"

"But, Warren, the things she says are all so weird and mixed up. Sometimes she talks of things that happened just recently and then again she babbles of things that took place a long time ago when we were kids. Once when the nurse came into the room, Helen began crying as though her heart would break and begged that we wouldn't think too harshly of her. Again she repeated over and over, 'He didn't do it—He didn't do it!'"

"Her other fears," I replied, "probably had to do with Woods. But that cry to Jim to 'Look out!' is a real clue and I'm going to sift it to the bottom."

"What are you going to do?" Mary demanded.

"I'm going to accuse Zalnitch of Jim's murder—going to accuse him to his face."

"Oh, be careful, Bupps! Nothing must happen to you!"

The tone she used, her sweet anxiety for my safety, went to my head and I reached out to take her in my arms, but with a little protesting gesture she stopped me.

"Please don't be foolish, Warren!" Then as she saw my spirits droop, she added, "Not till Helen is well."

10

I Accuse Zalnitch

Mr. Zalnitch is busy and can't see you."

The girl, evidently a stenographer or secretary, looked coolly competent in her white shirt-waist and well-made skirt. I was surprised to find a young woman of her evident education and refinement in the employ of such a man.

"Did you give him my message?" I asked.

"Yes. He said he was not interested."

I felt vaguely disappointed that my strategy had not worked. I had given the name of Anderson, and had represented myself as the head of the Steamfitters' Union of Cleveland, anxious for instructions on how to settle a labor problem in our local union. I had done this, feeling that if I gave my own name, he might refuse to see me. Apparently my alias was to have no better success.

"When will he be free, can you tell me?"

"I couldn't say," the girl answered. "He is very busy at present, but if you will come in and wait, perhaps he may see you later."

It seemed to me there was the faintest suggestion of a smile on the girl's face as I stepped across the threshold into the small waiting-room, but I hadn't a chance to observe more closely, for she turned her back on me at once and immediately resumed her typewriting.

The room in which I found myself was one of a dingy suite in an old warehouse that had been converted into a newspaper building to house *The Uplift*, a weekly paper, edited by a Russian Jew named Borsky and financed by Schreiber. It was a typical anarchistic sheet, and had been suppressed for a time, during the war. Opposite where I sat was a door from which the paint had peeled in places. This evidently led into Zalnitch's office, for I could hear the murmur of voices behind it. The rooms were ill-lighted and unclean, and it made me mad to see as nice a girl as the stenographer working herself to death in such dingy surroundings and for such a man as Zalnitch.

I watched her as she worked and marveled that any one could make her fingers go so rapidly. I noticed with admiration and dissatisfaction, that unlike my stenographers, she didn't have to stop to erase a misspelled word every two minutes. I wondered what salary Zalnitch paid her and if she would like to change employers.

"I hope you will pardon my interrupting your work—" I began.

"You're not," the girl responded, without even glancing up.

"May I ask if you are entirely satisfied with your employment here?"

"Why do you ask?" she inquired, stopping for a moment and fixing me with clear gray eyes.

"I am badly in need of a competent stenographer and I thought you might prefer working in a place where the surroundings are pleasanter and the pay probably higher."

She studied me a moment, as though card-indexing me, then having apparently decided that I was in earnest and not merely trying to flirt, that elusive smile again played about her mouth.

"You are the first steamfitter I ever met that found himself badly in need of a stenographer."

Caught! I bit my lip at my stupid blunder, but had to laugh in spite of myself.

"Your make-up is all wrong, Mr. Anderson—if your name is Anderson. I don't know what you are trying to do, nor why you picked out steamfitting as your mythical life-work, but I do know you aren't a detective."

This time the smile came out in the open. I liked her immensely. She might make an ally.

She would at least know what had happened in the office during the last few days.

"Miss—?"

"Miller," she added.

"Miss Miller. I am a lawyer, and my sister is about to be accused of a terrible crime which she didn't commit. I think I know who did commit it, but so far I haven't been able to connect him definitely with the crime. I think you can help me. Will you?"

"What makes you think I can help you?" she asked.

"Because you are so situated you can observe the person I believe to be responsible for the crime," I replied.

Her gaze changed from pleasant questioning to indignant surprise. When she spoke her voice was coldly final.

"I think you have made a mistake in judgment of character. Please let me finish my work now."

"Miss Miller, please don't think for a minute that I—"

Behind me a door opened and, as I turned, I found myself looking into the wrathful eyes of a stunted little man with an enormous head. Any one who has once seen Zalnitch can never forget him. His wizened, misshapen body is a grotesque caricature of a man's, which, surmounted by his huge head with its bushy hair, makes him look for all the world like some scientist's experiment. In the doorway to Zalnitch's private office stood Schreiber, a heavy-jowled, unsmiling mastiff of a man.

"What do you want that you should be keeping my stenographer from working?" Zalnitch's voice rose in a shrill crescendo. "Get out of here! You have no business here. Get out!"

"Zalnitch, I came here to speak to you."

"Get out!" he screamed. "I won't talk with you. I have no time to waste, even if you have. I know who you are. You're the brother-in-law of Felderson, the blood-sucking millionaire who sent me to jail. I won't talk with you, do you hear?"

As he grew more excited I seemed to grow cooler.

"Zalnitch, I'm going to swear out a warrant against you for my brother's murder."

For a moment the little man blinked at me in amazement; then he threw back his head and laughed, a shrill, giggling squeak. With his fists he pounded his misshapen legs.

"You arrest me for his murder? Hee-hee! You hear, Schreiber? He is going to—to arrest me!"

Suddenly he stopped, as quickly as he had started.

"Go ahead! Arrest me! Try to send me to prison again. I'll make you sweat blood before you are through. You think I killed him—your brother? I wish I had. I'd be proud to say I killed him! You hear? I wish I had killed him. I wish he were alive so I *could* kill him."

The little monstrosity emphasized each of his staccato sentences by stamping a puny foot on the floor. His gloating over Jim's death was more than flesh could stand.

"Stop!" I yelled. "If it wasn't you that killed him, it was one of that murderous gang of cutthroats and anarchists that was with you. If it wasn't you, then it was Schreiber's son—that Prussian jail-bird, or one of his friends."

Zalnitch's eyes blazed. "You call us anarchists and cutthroats. You, who are a product of the rotten government that has ground down and oppressed the people I represent. Because we rebel, you throw us in prison, making a mockery of your boasted liberty. So they did for a time in Russia. You call us 'cutthroats.' It's a good term. I hope to God we earn that title."

Finding that the talk was turning into a political harangue, I turned my back on Zalnitch and started toward the door. Schreiber followed me.

"Chust one minud." There was heavy menace in his look. "You galled my son a chail-bird a minud ago. He vas in chail because he did righd, but dot don't matter. You're egsited, because your brodder vas gilled. Ve don't know nodding aboud it. Ve heard aboud it de nexd day. I don'd have nodding against Velderson, bud if you dry to pud my son, Karl, in chail again, someding vill happen to you. I'm delling dis to you vor your own good."

Disappointed at the interview, I closed the door behind me and started down the hall. I don't know just what I had hoped to find out, but I thought Zalnitch would betray himself in some way—must in some way show his guilty knowledge of Jim's death. Instead, he had laughed at me when I threatened to arrest him, even wished he could claim the credit for the crime.

I heard the pattering of feet and turned to find Miss Miller behind me.

"Mr. Thompson."

"Yes, Miss Miller."

"A few moments ago you asked me to help you discover who killed your brother-in-law. For some reason you think Mr. Zalnitch had something to do with it, and you wanted me to give you any information I could about him."

"Yes," I responded.

"When you made that proposal, I was very angry because I resented your thinking I'd spy on my employer. However, your suspicions are so ridiculous I feel it is only fair to tell you that you are wasting your time."

"What makes you so sure that Zalnitch had nothing to do with it, Miss Miller?"

"Because I know he is utterly incapable of doing anything of that kind," she answered.

I half smiled. "Mr. Zalnitch has the reputation of holding life very cheaply—that is, the lives of others who stand in his way. He hated my brother-in-law for that very reason. If he didn't kill him, it wasn't because he didn't want to. For proof of it, you heard what he said in there."

The girl looked me over for a minute. A far-away look had come into her eyes.

"Mr. Thompson, Mr. Zalnitch is obsessed by a wonderful idea. You people call him 'Bolshevist' and 'anarchist,' because he is trying to overthrow the existing order of things. In working out his great theory, he would stamp out a nation if it interfered with the fulfillment of his plan, and he would not think that he had done anything wrong. In fact, he would think it the only thing to do. In that much, he holds life cheaply. But if you think he would descend to wreaking vengeance on individuals for personal spite, you are all wrong. He is too big a man for that."

"Did Zalnitch send you out to say this to me?" I asked suspiciously.

The girl flushed angrily. "Really, Mr. Thompson, you make it almost impossible for any one to help you. Instead of being sent, I may be dismissed for having come out here to talk to you. You asked for my assistance and now that I have tried to give it, you make me regret the impulse."

She turned and started to leave, but I called her back.

"Miss Miller, please forgive me and don't think me ungrateful. Mr. Felderson meant more to me than any person living, and I have made up by mind to bring his murderer to justice if I have to devote the rest of my life to it. I know that I have been jumping at conclusions. I've done a lot of things since Mr. Felderson's death that I can't understand, myself,—things that were entirely unlike me—but I feel that I would be a traitor to my brother-in-law's memory unless I follow every possible clue. He had only three enemies and one was Zalnitch, who threatened him. Isn't it only natural that I should suspect him?"

Her look was entirely sympathetic as she replied.

"I know how Mr. Felderson's death must have affected you, Mr. Thompson, and I do want to help you. You say he had three enemies; then I advise you to look for the other two, for I am positive Mr. Zalnitch had nothing to do with the murder."

I thanked her and went down the rickety stairs, believing somehow that she had told me the truth. But if not Zalnitch, then who? I knew that in less than a week, as soon as Helen was well enough to stand the shock, she would be indicted, unless in the meantime, I could discover the murderer. Helen had regained consciousness the night before, but was far too weak to undergo any questioning. My impatience at the delay, necessary before she could tell the story of the crime, had driven me, most foolishly, I now realized, into trying to force Zalnitch to a guilty admission of complicity.

When I got hold of myself, I knew well enough that the only sensible course was to wait until Helen should be able to clear up the mystery, so I went to the office and began the heavy task of putting Jim's effects in order.

11

A Double Indictment

J im was buried on Tuesday. The funeral was very quiet, only Mary and myself, with a few of Jim's most intimate friends, attending. I have always had a repugnance to large and ostentatious funerals and I felt that Jim would have preferred to have the actual ceremony over as quickly and quietly as possible. It affected me too much to allow me to think of anything else but my loss, at the time, and I should have left town the day after, had I not received a summons to appear before the grand jury.

Mary called me up and told me that she, too, had been summoned, so I drove the car around for her. She was nervous and frightened at the thought of having to testify and she asked me all the questions she could think of on what to do and what to say. I reassured her, telling her the district attorney was friendly to Jim and that I was confident our testimony as to Helen's words would stave off any indictment until Helen was well enough to testify.

"But, Warren, the fact that she was delirious will make it pretty shaky testimony, won't it?" Mary argued.

"Yes, that's true. But I don't think that they will want to bring an indictment while Helen is ill. You see, the indictment couldn't be served anyway, and I think our testimony will convince them there's a reasonable doubt as to Helen's guilt."

She seemed convinced until the gloomy bulk of the court-house came in view, when terror rushed back fourfold.

"Oh, Bupps, can't I get out of it?"

"No, dear, it's got to be gone through with. Remember it depends on you and me."

"But what if they ask me Jim's and Helen's conversation before they started for the country-club?"

"Tell them as little as possible, but stick to the truth. We know Helen's innocent and the truth can't hurt her."

We passed Inspector Robinson in the hall down-stairs and the half smile on his lips irritated me. It was his report to the grand jury that had stirred things up. He knew only too well that with the sensational *Sun* to back him, an indictment would be taken by the public to mean proven guilt.

At the entrance to the anteroom we found Wicks, his face drawn into lines of the most acute misery.

"I couldn't 'elp it, sir. They made me come."

"I know it, Wicks. Don't worry! It's a mere formality," I reassured him.

"I 'ope so, sir, but I don't like it."

"None of us do, Wicks, but it can't be helped," I replied. "Did Annie come with you?"

"No, sir. Strange to say she wasn't called, sir."

Good! That helped our case some. Mary and I walked into the anteroom to await our turn. The coroner was already there. Wicks had followed us and took a seat close by. Mary's face was a study in suppressed nervousness.

"Couldn't you go in there with me, Bupps?" she asked.

"No, Mary, the grand jury does its work in secret."

A clerk called the coroner and as he passed from the room, Robinson and Pickering came in. Robinson didn't even glance in my direction, but Pickering walked over quickly and shook hands.

"Devilish sorry things have taken the turn they have, old man," he said.

"You mean about—my sister?"

"Yes. Robinson seems to think he has all the proof he needs. I wish I could help you."

"Thanks awfully," I replied.

He had only been seated a few moments when he was called to testify. As the coroner left the room, I tried to read in his face the nature of his testimony, but it was inscrutable. Pickering was out in less than ten minutes, and then Wicks was called. His legs seemed a bit shaky as he started for the door and he gave me a parting look, half awe, half terror.

Robinson paced up and down, his short stubby legs expressing confidence and satisfaction. Every turn, he scrutinized Mary, as if trying to place her in some criminal category.

At last Wicks came out, perspiring as if he'd been in a steam bath. Robinson looked him over once, gave a snort of derision and passed into the jury room. I wanted to ask Wicks some questions, but the poor man fled before I could attract his notice.

Mary got up and walked over to the big windows where a flood of warm September sunlight poured into the room. For a moment she stood gazing down on the crowded square below, then suddenly turned and half sobbed:

"Bupps, I can't stand it! I may say something that will hurt Helen."

Great sobs shook her slender body. I went over and clumsily tried to comfort her.

"Mary, dear, Helen didn't do it. When she is well enough, we'll be able to find out all about it. Even if they do bring an indictment, Helen can prove her innocence."

The sobs diminished to sniffles, and then to occasional sighs. She opened her bag, extracted a miniature powder-puff and dabbed at her small upturned nose spitefully. I knew that the storm had passed.

"I know—that—that I'm foolish to c-cry, but I just c-couldn't help it."

A clerk opened the door and called Mary's name. She gave me a startled glance and her face blanched. I thought she was going to break down again, but suddenly I saw her raise her chin defiantly and an angry sparkle come to her eyes. She snapped shut her vanity-bag and marched toward the jury room like a soldier, sentenced to be shot, yet determined to die bravely.

It was only after she had left that I began to think about my own testimony. After all, the evidence was terrifyingly strong against Helen. She had threatened to kill Jim. She had quarreled with him just before their last ride, had chosen the back seat purposely, had Jim's revolver with her, and knew she was being taken to see her lover humiliated and threatened. Against all this, I had only a brother's faith in his sister and those half dozen words cried out in a delirium. A sickening certainty that they would indict Helen came over me. What if she did—? What if she should confess?

In some way I had to save Helen if only for mother's sake. After all, Woods, too, had threatened Jim. He knew Jim had proof of his dishonesty. He had made the engagement and had asked Jim to come alone. At this point of my review of the facts I decided to tell the jury all. If Woods was at the country-club the entire evening he would be able to establish a complete alibi and my testimony would not hurt him, while it might be enough, if I could make it so, to hold the jury until Helen could testify. Hearing steps outside, I turned to see the object of my mental attentions walk into the room.

"You here, Woods?" I queried.

"Yes. Those admirable servants of your sister's gave the police just enough of the vulgar details of that meeting between Felderson and myself to make them think I—well, they ordered me to report and here I am."

He looked worried and irritable. For the first time I realized what the man must have gone through during the last few days, with his business troubles and Helen's injury. How he had met his obligations without Helen's money, I didn't know.

"I should have thought you'd have been glad to testify to save Helen from an indictment."

Woods whirled around. "You don't mean to say there's a chance of that, Thompson? Why, she didn't do it, she couldn't have done it. She—she isn't capable of doing such a thing. It's monstrous. I've read the rot that *The Sun* has been printing, but I didn't think—I can't think any one would take it seriously." A gray shadow seemed to fall across his face.

"Felderson was shot from behind and Helen was the only one with him," I threw out, watching Woods closely to see what effect my words would have on him. The man looked as though he knew more about the crime than I had supposed.

"I know that! But haven't people sense enough to see that Helen is utterly incapable of such an act. Good God, they must be blind!"

I was brought back to the business on hand by hearing my name shouted. They must have let Mary out by another door for when I entered the jury room she was not there. It was hot and stuffy, smelling of stale tobacco and staler clothing. I noticed that the jurymen seemed deeply interested and that they were, for the most part, a rather intelligent lot. The foreman, a near-sighted business-looking person, seemed to radiate sympathy through his glasses. The district attorney, Kirkpatrick, knew Jim well, had his help often and was one of his best friends.

"What is your name?" he asked.

"Warren Thompson."

"Your address?"

"Eleven thirty-two Grant Avenue."

"Your business?"

"I am a lawyer," I responded.

The district attorney seated himself at a table and arranged some papers before him.

"You were what relation to the deceased?"

"The brother-in-law," I replied.

"Mr. Thompson," the attorney began, leaning on the table in front of him, "will you please tell the jury if there was any unhappiness in the married life of your sister and brother-in-law?"

"Until recently Mr. and Mrs. Felderson were very happy together. During the last three months their happiness has not been quite—so pronounced."

"What was the cause of their disagreement?" I determined to begin my attack on Woods at once.

"A man whom Mr. Felderson disliked and did not wish to come to the house."

"Can you tell the jury that man's name?"

"Frank Woods."

The attorney glanced at his notes.

"Did this man Woods make love to Mrs. Felderson?"

"I couldn't say. He was very attentive to her."

"Did Mrs. Felderson ask her husband to divorce her?"

"Yes," I replied.

"And Mr. Felderson refused?"

"No. Mr. Felderson consented."

"You are sure of that?" he demanded.

"Yes. I was present when he said he would give her a divorce."

"Was Woods there at the time?"

"Yes."

The foreman of the jury interrupted here.

"Will you tell the jury just what took place at that meeting?"

I told them briefly what happened, not forgetting to mention that Woods had threatened Jim's life in case he did not let Helen go.

"Has that man been summoned?" asked the foreman.

"Yes. He is waiting to appear now," a clerk responded.

"Mr. Thompson, did you hear your sister threaten to kill her husband?" Kirkpatrick asked.

"My sister was very excited at that time and said several things—"

"Please answer my question!" fired the district attorney.

"I can't remember," I replied. Kirkpatrick again consulted his papers.

"A witness says that on the evening of the disagreement between Mr. and Mrs. Felderson, she used the words: 'I could kill him,' referring to her husband. Did you hear her use those words?"

"I don't think she realized what she was saying."

"I did not ask for your opinions. Did you hear her say she could kill him or that she would like to kill him?"

"Yes."

The attorney seemed satisfied and I noticed the foreman of the jury lean back in his chair.

"Now, Mr. Thompson," Kirkpatrick began, "on the evening of the tragedy did you see Mrs. Felderson leave with Mr. Felderson?"

"No," I replied.

"Do you know if she was sitting in the back seat or the front seat of that automobile?" he asked.

"I couldn't say."

Kirkpatrick took Jim's revolver from the table.

"Is this revolver familiar to you?"

"I don't know."

"Did Mr. Felderson have a revolver like this?" he demanded.

"Yes."

"Do you know whether he was carrying it at the time of the tragedy?"

"I'm not sure," I stated.

"Did Mr. Felderson usually carry a gun?"

"No."

"Did Mrs. Felderson have a revolver?"

"No," I replied, "I don't think she even knows how to use one."

"Please only answer my questions!" Kirkpatrick rebuked me sharply.

"You have stated to the jury that Mr. Woods had threatened Mr. Felderson's life in case he did not give Mrs. Felderson a divorce.

When did Mr. Felderson intend giving his wife the promised divorce?"

"I don't think he really intended to give Mrs. Felderson a divorce."

"But you stated that he consented to a divorce?"

"He did, but with certain reservations," I answered.

"What were those reservations?"

"That there should be nothing in Mr. Woods' past that could cause Mrs. Felderson trouble in the future, in case she married Woods."

"Did Mr. Woods know of Mr. Felderson's intention not to divorce Mrs. Felderson?" he demanded.

"I don't know. I know that Mr. Felderson had made an important discovery about Mr.

Woods' past life."

"Was this discovery of such a nature as to cause Mr. Felderson to refuse a divorce?"

"It was!" I answered.

"Can you tell the jury what this discovery was?"

"No, I can not."

"Did Mr. Woods know that Mr. Felderson had made this discovery?"

"I think he did."

"Aren't you certain?"

"No."

"This is important, Mr. Thompson. Will you tell the jury why you think Mr. Woods knew of Mr. Felderson's discovery?"

"Because Mr. Woods called Mr. Felderson up shortly after the discovery was made and asked for an interview at the country-club."

"Was Mr. Felderson on his way to that meeting when he met his death?" the attorney queried.

"Yes," I responded.

"Do you know whether Mr. Felderson intended to inform Woods that he would not divorce Mrs. Felderson?"

"I think he intended to accuse Woods of dishonesty," I replied.

"Mrs. Felderson knew the purpose of the meeting, did she not?"

"I couldn't say."

Kirkpatrick turned to the jury.

"Has the jury any questions they wish to ask?"

I seized my opportunity.

"I would like to say a few words with the permission of the jury."

Receiving a nod of consent, I related to them as briefly as possible my conviction of my sister's innocence, her cry of danger to her husband, and the coincidence of the black limousine on the road at about the same time as the tragedy. I also told of the enmity of Zalnitch for Jim and of his presence with the others in the black limousine. The foreman of the jury leaned forward.

"Will you repeat the words that your sister uttered?"

"She cried, 'Look out, Jim! It's going to hit us!'"

"Your sister was delirious at the time, was she not?"

"Yes," I answered. "But from the tone of her voice I feel perfectly sure she referred to something that occurred on the night of the tragedy."

"You think she referred to the black limousine when she said, 'It's going to hit us'?" the foreman continued.

"Yes."

"Yet the coroner's verdict was that your brother-in-law was killed by a bullet, fired, apparently, from behind and above."

I felt the weakness of my ground.

"The bullet might have been fired from the automobile and ricochetted from some part of Mr. Felderson's machine."

I saw the incredible smile that played on the face of the prosecutor.

"That will do, Mr. Thompson," Kirkpatrick announced, and I passed out of the stuffy room into the corridor. Wicks had returned and was standing with Mary. They looked at me with wide and anxious eyes.

Mary saw the droop in my shoulders and caught my arm.

"What happened, Warren?" she asked.

"Nothing yet," I responded.

"Are they going to——?"

"I don't know, I don't know."

Tears welled up in Mary's eyes. "Oh, Warren, that man was terrible!"

"What man?" I asked.

"The man who asked me all the questions," Mary sobbed. "There wasn't anything he didn't ask me."

"Did he ask you about the conversation between Helen and Jim?"

"He asked me everything, I tell you!" Mary exclaimed angrily. "He twisted and turned everything I said into something horrible."

Discouraged, I led the way to the car. I drove out into the country, thinking the fresh air might quiet Mary's nerves. Twice I tried to start a conversation about some trivial thing, to take her mind off her unpleasant experience of the afternoon, but with no success. It always came back to the jury room. Our drive, for the most part, was a silent one. At length we turned back and as we walked up the steps of Mary's home, her father came from the house with a newspaper in his hand.

"This is terrible, Warren."

"What is it?" I cried, reaching for the sheet.

It was an extra edition of *The Press*, our only respectable paper. In black head-lines, I read the words:

SOCIETY LEADER INDICTED FOR HUSBAND'S MURDER!

Then underneath in small type:

Frank Woods, Well Known Business Man, Released on $10,000 Bail.

Helen and Frank Woods had both been indicted.

12

Who Am I?

I jumped into the automobile and drove as fast as I could to the offices of Simpson and Todd, the best criminal lawyers in the state, to retain them as council for Helen. Simpson had already gone home, but George Todd was there, and I talked the case over with him.

"You can get a stay of proceedings, can't you?" I asked.

"Surely," he replied. "I'll see that the warrant isn't served until Mrs. Felderson's doctor assures me she is out of danger. The trial needn't come off for three or four months—six if you wish. We can see to that. In the meantime, when will you be able to see Mrs. Felderson?"

"I was going up there now," I answered. "The chances are the doctor won't let me question her yet, but it may be we can see her. Will you come with me?"

"I'd like very much to. Wait till I get my coat!"

We ran up to the hospital and asked if we could be admitted if only for a few moments to Mrs. Felderson's room. Johnson, the little intern with the glasses, had just come in, and when he heard my request he was splutteringly indignant.

"What the devil do you think Mrs. Felderson is suffering from, a broken ankle? Don't you realize she has been desperately ill? If you tried to question her now, she'd become excited and it might result in a serious relapse. Of course you can't see her! You won't be able to talk to her for two or three weeks yet."

"I'm sorry," I said, "I should have known better. It was stupid of me, but then, I've been little else than stupid for days. This tragedy has been too much for me. You will let me know as soon as she can be seen, won't you, Johnson?"

"I'll let you know," he murmured. "You may be able to *see* her to-morrow, but I won't let you bother her with any infernal questions until she is well."

The week passed only too slowly. Each day I went to the hospital and sat for a brief fifteen or twenty minutes by Helen's side. She was fully conscious and I thought I could see at times that there were questions she wanted to ask me. Remembering the doctor's emphatic instructions, I said very little, never asking any questions, only telling her a few of the unimportant happenings of the town. She seemed uninterested and lay apathetically quiescent except when some apparently perplexing question corrugated her brows. They told her of Jim's death early in the week, but far from being shocked, she had appeared almost indifferent, showing only too plainly how little he meant in her life. Woods she never referred to.

Mary, of course, was her devoted slave, hardly leaving her bedside, and in our daily meetings at the hospital, I fell more and more in love with her, if such a thing were possible. Once when I was coming up the corridor with a large bunch of flowers, I met her outside Helen's door. As she took the blooms from me, she reached up and patted my cheek.

"Bupps, you're a darling to bring these lovely flowers to Helen every day. I think you're quite the nicest brother a girl could have."

"If you think that, why won't you have me?" I asked.

"I think I will——" she answered, smiling, "for a brother."

She started to open the door, but I grasped her hand.

"Mary, do be serious! You know I love you."

She haughtily drew herself up in all the majesty of her five feet three inches and commanded: "Unhand me, villain! I spurn your tempting offer." Then earnestly, "Let me go, Bupps! I've got to put these flowers away."

With a quick wrench she freed herself and was gone, leaving me half sick with love of her.

After the first sensational extra, the newspapers had said but little of Helen's and Frank's indictment. Somehow I was confident that Helen would be able to clear herself. Woods had published a statement in which he said he would be able to prove where he was every minute of the evening of the tragedy, and so had had no difficulty in finding bail. In fact, since the indictment, he seemed to have gained a good deal of sympathy and popularity. Every one who knew of his devotion to Helen felt that he had indicted himself to try to save her.

One morning, about a week after my interview with the be-spectacled intern, I met Doctor Forbes as he was coming from Helen's room and he gave me permission to ask her a few questions.

"I'm trusting to your good sense, Thompson, not to overdo it," Forbes cautioned. "Remember, she is still in a very weak condition and don't be surprised if she fails to respond to your questions as you expect. Above all things, do not refer in any way to the fact that she has been indicted, the shock might be too much for her."

"Thank you, Doctor," I replied, eager to get away, "I'll be very careful."

"And remember, no more than ten minutes this first time."

I nodded and opened the door. Helen was propped up in bed and showed unmistakably the great suffering she had been through. She was pale and wan, but smiled when she saw me and gave me her cheek to kiss.

"Good morning," she whispered. "The flowers were lovely."

"I'm glad you liked them, Sis, dear," I said, sitting down by the side of her bed.

I asked her the usual questions, how she felt and if she wanted anything, and then tried to lead up to the only question that was of any consequence to either of us.

"Helen, dear, there are certain questions about your accident that have puzzled us. The doctor said that you could talk for ten minutes this morning and I want to ask you some questions."

"Wait a minute!" she interrupted. "Did the doctor say I might really talk this morning?"

"Yes, dear."

"There are a hundred questions then that you must answer me. I want to know so many things." She looked away and passed a thin hand over her forehead. Finally she turned her big brown eyes toward me and said:

"First, tell me who I am!"

For a brief second I felt numb all through. My brain whirled until I thought my head would burst.

"Helen, dear, what did you say?"

My speech was thick, as though my tongue was swollen. Still keeping her gaze fixed on me, she continued:

"They call me Helen, and I gather that you are my brother. There is a beautiful girl who comes here every day. She and I seem to be great friends, but I don't know her, I have heard them call her Mary; tell me who she is!"

If I could have run from the room I should have done so. A horror gripped me such as I never felt before. Then I saw two large tears tremble in Helen's eyes, overflow and course down her cheeks and I gathered all the strength that I could muster for the task of trying to awaken a memory that had apparently ceased to function.

"Helen, dearest little sister, I am your brother. The beautiful girl you speak of is Mary Pendleton, one of the best and truest friends you ever had. She was your bridesmaid, don't you remember?"

Helen shook her head weakly.

"I have been married, then?" she asked.

"You were married to James Felderson. Can't you remember him?" I begged.

Again she shook her head. "No. It's all gone." She thought hard a minute, then she asked: "He is dead—my husband?"

"Yes," I muttered, trying to keep the tears back, "he was killed in the same accident—"

"What was he like?" she interrupted.

"Helen, think!" I cried, fighting blindly against the terror that was choking me. "Little sister. You must think—*hard*. Jim. Don't you remember big handsome Jim?" I snatched my watch from my pocket and opened the back, where I carried a small picture of Jim, taken years before. I had put it there in boyish admiration when I first knew him. I held it up in front of her eyes. "You must remember him, Helen!"

She gazed at the picture with eyes in which there were tears and a little fright, but not a spark of recognition. Fearing that I was over-exciting her, I sat close to her and drew as best I could a mental picture of Jim. I was only half-way through the recital when the door opened and Doctor Forbes came in.

"The ten minutes are up, Mr. Thompson."

I stooped and kissed Helen.

"Promise that you'll come back to-morrow," she whispered.

I promised and hurried from the room. Outside the doctor awaited me questioningly.

"Her memory is completely gone!" I gasped.

The doctor patted me on the shoulder sympathetically.

"We suspected that day before yesterday. I would have told you before, but thought that your questions might start her memory functioning."

I gripped him by both arms. "But, Doctor, can nothing be done? Will she have to—have to begin all over again?"

"I can't say yet. There may be some pressure there still. We'll have to wait until she is much stronger before we can tell."

13

WE PLAN THE DEFENSE

H elen's loss of memory was the last straw. The shock of finding her unable to remember the most familiar things was bad enough from a purely physical standpoint, but when I realized how completely it swept away all my plans for Helen's defense, how it fastened the guilt on her poor shoulders, I felt that our case was hopeless indeed.

I drove to the offices of Simpson and Todd and was lucky enough to find both of them in. Simpson, a slender man with steel-gray hair and eyes, at once ordered a closed session to thrash out the whole affair. He first made me repeat everything I knew about Jim's murder, from the beginning. Several times he interrupted me, to ask a question, but for the most part he sat with his back to me, gazing out of the window, the tips of his fingers to his lips. Half the time I thought he wasn't listening, until a quick question would show his interest. Todd, on the contrary, was the picture of attention. He took notes in shorthand most of the time I was talking. When I had finished, Simpson rose and came over to me.

"Let's examine this thing from the start. You have three people who had a motive for killing Felderson—Zalnitch, Woods and Mrs. Felderson. Let's take Zalnitch first, for I think suspicion falls the slightest on him. You say that Felderson helped to convict Zalnitch in the Yellow Pier case and that he made vague threats against those who had put him in prison, after he was released. Good! There's a motive and a threat. He was seen on the same road that Mr. Felderson traveled, a short time before the murder. All those facts point to Zalnitch's complicity. But—the bullet that killed Felderson was fired from behind and above, according to the coroner's statement. Knowing the average juryman, I should say that we would have to stretch things pretty far to make him believe that a shot fired from one rapidly moving automobile at another rapidly moving automobile would ricochet and kill a man. That's asking a little too much. Also, it is hard to believe that Schreiber, who was driving the car, would risk a smash-up to his own car and possible death for himself and party, in order to try to make Felderson go into the ditch. Then, too, if Zalnitch recognized Felderson's car, why didn't he fire point-blank at Felderson instead of waiting till he got past? No! The case against Zalnitch falls down. We can strike him off the list."

I hated to give him up, but I had to admit Simpson's logic was faultless.

"Now let us take up the case of Woods. Here is a man who threatened Felderson's life unless he gave his wife a divorce, which you say Felderson did not intend to do. There, again, is a motive. Woods knew that Felderson was in possession of certain papers that would ruin him. There is a stronger motive." He turned to me. "By the way, you have those papers, haven't you?"

I hadn't thought of them until that very minute.

"I don't know where they are right now, but I'm pretty sure I can find them."

He nodded.

"Get hold of them by all means! They may be important to us." He lit a cigar and threw himself into a chair.

"Well, let's go on. Woods had all the motive necessary for killing Felderson. He made a definite engagement with Felderson on the night of the murder, to meet him at a certain time and place specified by Woods. That's important. Everything up to that point is as clear as crystal, yet you say you have positive testimony that Woods was at the country-club waiting for Felderson at about the time the murder took place, and Woods claims that he has an absolute alibi. If that is true, it lets him out."

"But I'm not sure he was at the country-club at the time the murder took place," I explained. "I only know he was there just before and just afterward."

"What do you know of his movements that night?" Simpson asked.

"I know he dined there at seven-thirty or thereabouts and that he ordered a drink at eight twenty-five."

"And what time was the murder?"

"Probably about a quarter past eight—the bodies were found at half past, they say," I answered.

Simpson shook his head. "I'm afraid his alibi is good. It's cutting things too fine to think that he could have run six miles and back in less than half an hour and committed a murder in the bargain. It would have taken a speedy automobile. Do you know whether he had an automobile that night?" he queried.

"I think he did. I can find out in a minute," I added, going to the telephone.

I called up the country-club and finally succeeded in getting Jackson on the wire. Jackson thought Mr. Woods did not have an automobile that night, because he had gone to town in Mr. Paisley's car.

"He might have used somebody else's car," Todd suggested.

Simpson shook his head again. "We're getting clear off the track, now."

An idea came to me suddenly and I called Up Pickering at the Benefit Insurance Company.

"This is Thompson speaking, Pickering," I said.

"Yes."

"Do you remember if an automobile passed you on the night of the Felderson murder, going toward the country-club?"

"No."

"Do you mean you don't remember?"

"No, I remember perfectly. There was only one automobile passed us and that was the black limousine."

"You're sure?" I asked.

"I'm positive, old man. We only saw one car from the time we left Blandesville, until we reached the city."

I put up the receiver and sank back in my chair.

"Well?" Todd flung at me.

"I'm out of luck!" I responded.

Simpson rose. "Let's go on. We have crossed off two of our suspects from the list, let's see—"

"I'd rather not go on," I interrupted, looking out of the window to escape Todd's searching eyes. There was a moment's silence, then Simpson spoke.

"We'll do our best but it will be a hard fight. If Mrs. Felderson could only recall what happened that night and before, we might have a chance, but every woman that has come up for murder during the last few years, has worked that lost memory gag."

"But my sister really *has* lost her memory!" I exclaimed.

"I know, my dear boy," Simpson soothed. "That is what makes it so difficult. If she were only shamming now, we could—. But with your sister as helpless as a child, the prosecuting attorney will so confuse her, that our case will be lost as soon as she takes the stand."

"Why put her on at all?" I asked.

"Because we have to, if we hope to win our case," he replied. "The one big chance to win your jury comes when your beautiful client testifies."

For a few minutes he was silent, obviously thinking, and thinking hard.

"Of course, our defense will have to be temporary insanity," he declared at last.

"Oh, not that!" I begged.

"It's our only chance," Simpson argued, "and I don't mind saying that it's a pretty poor chance at that. Three years ago it might have been all right, because a conviction only meant a few months at a fashionable sanitarium, and then freedom. But when that Truesdale woman went free, an awful howl went up all over the country and I'm afraid the next woman who is found, 'guilty but insane,' will be sent to a real asylum."

A shudder of horror ran through me. For Helen to be sent to an asylum while her mind was in its weak state might well mean permanent insanity.

"You talk to your sister as often as you can and try to help her recover her lost memory. Of course you'll have the best specialists examine and prescribe for her. In the meantime, we'll investigate both the Woods and Zalnitch cases to see if they are hole-proof."

"You might get those papers on Woods, if you will," Todd reminded me.

I thanked them and left, greatly depressed but ready to fight to the last ditch to save Helen's life. The papers dealing with Woods had not been among Jim's effects when I had looked them over at the office and I was confident they had not been picked up on the night of the murder, for they would have been returned to me. Thinking they had probably been left in one of the pockets of the automobile, and overlooked when the machine was searched, I decided to run out to the Felderson home the first thing in the morning.

14

BULLETPROOF

Jim's car had been moved to his own garage the morning after the accident, and as I had a pass-key to the place I found it unnecessary to go to the house at all. Wicks and Annie were taking care of the establishment until Helen should come home, or the house be sold.

I opened the door of the garage and shuddered involuntarily as I caught sight of the wrecked Peckwith-Pierce. It had been more badly smashed than I had at first supposed. On the night of the murder I saw that the chassis was twisted and the axle broken, but I had not noticed what that jolting crash had done to the body of the car. The steering rod was broken and the cushions were caked with mud. One wheel sagged at a drunken angle like a lop-ear and the wind-shield was nothing but a mangled frame. One long gash ran the length of the body, as though it had scraped against a rock, and this gash ended in a jagged wound the size of a man's head. In the back were three small splintered holes.

I examined these with particular interest, wondering what could have caused them. Evidently the police had neglected to examine the machine. The sight of what looked like the end of a nail caused me to drop to my knees and to begin digging frantically at the wood with my pen-knife. At the end of five feverish minutes I held the prize in my hand.

It was a misshapen, steel, "32" rifle bullet.

In the floor of the car, near where Jim's feet must have been, I found two more splintered holes, apparently made by the same rifle from which the shots had been fired into the back of the car.

Two thoughts flashed through my mind, exuberant assurance that this latest discovery cleared Helen completely. She couldn't have fired a rifle from the rear seat of the automobile, nor could she have put those bullet holes into the back of the car. In my joy that I had found proof of my sister's innocence, I forgot to speculate on who could have committed the murder. My second thought was really a continuation of the first, that I must bring the coroner and Simpson at once to confirm my discovery.

I carefully locked the door of the garage, as though fearful some one would rob me of my find, or that the automobile might move away of its own volition, then I ran to the house and rang the bell. All the curtains were drawn and I had about decided there was no one at home, when, after what seemed an interminable wait, I heard the sound of footsteps within, and Wicks opened the door.

"Who'd you expect to see, Wicks, a policeman?" I asked.

"No, sir. One of those blarsted reporters, sir."

"Poor old Wicksy," I sympathized. "Well, it'll soon be over now. I want to use the telephone."

I ran down the hall to the table where I knew the telephone to be, and called up Simpson. He promised he would come right up.

The coroner demurred for a moment, pleading important business, but when he heard I had proof that would clear Mrs. Felderson, he, too, promised to be with me in a few minutes.

Wicks, who had been listening, was so excited that he momentarily forgot himself and clutched me by the arm as I put down the receiver.

"Is it true, sir, that you can prove Mrs. Felderson 'ad nothing to do with it?" he gasped.

"Truest thing you know, Wicks!"

"I fear I'm going to act unseemly, sir. I feel like yelling, 'ip, 'ip, sir." Then he noticed he had me by the arm and hastily murmured apology.

"That's all right, Wicksy, old top. Go as far as you like," I cried.

"I'm so happy and relieved I could kiss the Kaiser."

"You surely wouldn't do that, sir," Wicks reproved.

"All right, Wicks. I guess it's not being done this year."

The butler turned to leave but stopped at the door to say: "Mr. Woods called about a week ago, sir."

"What did he want?" I demanded.

"He stated as 'ow 'e was after some papers concerning a business deal that 'e and Mr. Felderson were interested in."

In the excitement over my discovery, I had completely forgotten the real errand that had brought me to the house.

"What did you tell him, Wicks?"

"I told 'im that you had charge of all Mr. Felderson's effects, sir, and that he could probably obtain them from you," the butler replied.

"That was right. Did he leave after that?"

"Shortly after that, sir," Wicks answered. "But first he asked for the key to the garage, sayin' that 'e would like to hinspect the auto."

"Did you give it to him?" I snapped.

"Y-yes, sir. I saw no 'arm in that, sir."

I ran to the garage and quickly searched the broad pockets of Jim's car. The portfolio was not there. I hurried toward the house to ask Wicks if Woods had had any papers with him when he returned the garage key, but slackened my pace before I had gone half-way. After all, it made very little difference. The evidence had only been gathered to keep Helen with her husband. Now, since that was no longer an issue, what did it matter if Woods had stolen the proofs of his own dishonesty. True, Simpson and Todd had asked me to get them, but I felt that they had urged the importance of those papers more to give me something to do than for any real need of them.

Just then an automobile came up the drive and Simpson jumped out. He was gravely skeptical until I led him into the garage and showed him the bullet holes; then he was enthusiastic. He examined the back of the car minutely, and at the end of his scrutiny he turned to me.

"I'm not at all sure that we were justified in giving Zalnitch a clean bill of health so soon. It is just possible he had a lot more to do with this than we supposed."

While we were talking the coroner drove up. He took the bullet I had extracted from the back of the car and looked at it as though he expected to find its owner's name etched on it, after which he examined the holes in the back of the car and in the foot-board. Then I eagerly related our suspicions against Zalnitch, but he shook his head.

"This would seem to clear Mrs. Felderson but it also makes it look as though every other suspect is innocent. Look at these holes in the floor! The bullets that lodged there must have been fired from above. Also you will notice there are three bullet holes in the back of the car and two in the foot-board, besides the shot that killed Mr. Felderson. Unless your friends, the Socialists, were carrying a young armory with them, they could never have fired that many shots in the short space of time that it took Mr. Felderson to pass them. I should say that it would take a man from—well, from fifteen to thirty seconds, at least, to fire six shots at *any* target, and before that time, the automobile would have been out of range."

"He might have used an automatic rifle," I interposed.

The coroner took off his hat and rubbed the bald spot on the back of his head.

"That is possible," he admitted, "but it doesn't explain how those bullet holes got into the floor. There might have been a struggle and the gun discharged into the floor that way."

"That doesn't explain the holes in the back of the car," I objected, fearing that they would again go back to the theory that Helen was responsible.

"The holes in the foot-board seem to me positive proof that the shots were fired from above," Simpson argued. "Are there any buildings or trees along that road where the murderer might have stationed himself and waited for Felderson to come along?"

"There are no buildings," I replied, "but there must be trees in the vicinity of that stream."

"That sounds as though it might bring results," Simpson said. "Thompson, suppose you take the coroner out there and see what you can find. In the meantime I'll start proceedings to quash that indictment against Mrs. Felderson."

The coroner insisted he was due at an inquest that very moment, but would go with me in the afternoon. As we walked toward the cars, Simpson asked me if I had found the papers dealing with Woods' case, and I told him I thought Woods had stolen them and repeated the information Wicks had given me.

"I don't think we shall need them, fortunately," Simpson replied. "Todd saw Woods last night. He's making a frantic effort to raise money and came to him, among others. He says that Woods can clear himself of all connection with the crime. Men who were with him that night can testify he didn't leave the club. By the way, Woods hasn't approached you, has he?"

"No," I laughed, "he knows I have no money, and if I had I wouldn't give it to him."

After they had left, I decided to go out to the Blandesville bridge and do a little preliminary scouting on my own. Eager for Mary's company, and wishing to tell her the glorious news that was to clear Helen, I drove to the hospital, only to find that Mary had not been there and Helen was asleep; so I drove on to Mary's, hoping to find her home.

"Miss Pendleton is just going out, but I will ask if she will see you," the maid informed me.

I stepped into the living-room and picked up a magazine. As I took it in my hand it fell open to a story entitled, "Who Murdered Merryvale?" I looked at one of the illustrations and quickly laid the magazine down, conscious that I'd never again read a mystery story built around a tragic death. Then I heard Mary's light step pattering down the stairs and turned to greet her. She was dressed in a smart, semi-military costume which she had worn while a volunteer chauffeur during the war, and she looked simply radiant.

"Mary, we've made certain discoveries which absolutely clear Helen of suspicion," I cried, taking her hands in mine. I told her of my find of the morning, and watched her eyes widen with joy and surprise. "So, while we haven't found out yet who murdered Jim, we know that Helen had no part in it."

Mary was thinking hard about something, but she recalled herself quickly, and said:

"Oh! It's wonderful, Bupps, simply *wonderful*!"

"I'm going out to the Blandesville bridge to do a little sleuthing on my own hook. Can you come with me?"

"I'm sorry, but I can't, Warren. I have another engagement," she answered.

"Some other man?" I asked, disappointed and a bit jealous.

"Yes."

"Is it that young Davis?"

She shook her head.

"It's some one you don't like very well."

"That's natural," I replied. "I don't love any of my rivals. Who is it?"

"Promise you won't say anything if I tell you who it is?"

"Of course I won't say anything," I said a little haughtily. "You have a perfect right to go with any one you care to."

"It's Frank Woods."

"Mary," I gasped, "do you mean to say you'd be seen with that man, after what he did to Jim?"

"Now, Bupps, you promised not to say anything."

"I know—but this is different. Do you think I'll stand quietly by and see that man make a fool of you as he did of Helen? Do you think I'll let that—that rake make love to you?"

"He's not going to make love to me!" Mary answered with some asperity.

"That's what you think. That's what Helen thought and Jim thought. That's what all of them think when he starts. Do you know what he wants to do? He asked you to go out with him so he could try to borrow money of you, to save his rotten hide."

"But, Bupps, he didn't ask me to go riding with him. I asked him to take me."

"You asked him to take you?" I cried.

"Don't talk so loud, Bupps! The people on the street will hear you."

If there was anything she could have said that would have made me angrier than I already was, it was that.

"I'm not talking loud," I shouted, "and what if I do? The people on the street may hear me, but they will *see* you with Frank Woods, which is a hundred times worse. Why, it is as much as a girl's reputation is worth to be seen alone with him."

"I'll take care of my reputation," she replied coldly.

"You think you will," I said, flinging myself into a chair.

"Warren! Do you know that's insulting?" Mary exclaimed angrily. "You're acting like a schoolboy. I have good reasons for wanting to go out with Frank Woods."

"Reasons!" I sneered.

She went into the hall and I followed.

"Mary, I don't know what your reasons are, and I don't care. I'm not going to have that man making love to you. Either you don't go out with him, or I quit."

Mary turned and looked me straight in the eyes.

"What do you mean?" she asked.

"Any girl who is Frank Woods' friend, after the mess he stirred up in my family, isn't my friend."

Mary's face was white, but her little chin was set determinedly.

"That's just as you wish," she said, and ran up-stairs.

I picked up my hat and gloves and left the house.

15

The Answer

The coroner and I drove out to the bridge that afternoon and I must admit I was mighty poor company. Mary's unreasonableness, her stupid obstinacy, when she knew she was wrong and I was right, her willingness to break our friendship at the first opportunity, gave me little room to think of anything else.

That she should risk her reputation to run after that man was inexplicable, but it was just like a woman. Show them a place they must not go or a man they must not see and they will sacrifice life, liberty and everybody else's happiness to satisfy their curiosity. It has been true from Pandora to Pankhurst.

Well, if she could get along without me, I could get along without her. I'm the easiest going person in the world, but when it comes to allowing the girl you are practically engaged to, to make a fool of herself over another man, I won't stand for it. I knew she would probably come to me afterward and say she was sorry and she didn't know, but I made up my mind that she would have to give me an awfully good reason for her sudden interest in Frank Woods before I would forgive her.

These thoughts held my attention all the way out. Now and again I would be recalled from my gloom by some question from the coroner. He was trying to solve the problem of who murdered Jim and I am sure he must have thought it strange that I was so preoccupied.

As we neared the bridge, I noticed again how scant the vegetation was on both sides of the road. Any one wishing to murder Jim would have been able to see him coming for at least a half-mile. On the left of the road was clay soil, sparsely covered with weeds and shrubs, while a half-mile away could be seen the thirteenth hole of the country-club golf links.

When we reached the crest of the hill leading down to the bridge, our eyes at once caught sight of a tall maple tree, on the right-hand side of the road and about two hundred yards from it.

As he saw it the coroner gave a grunt of satisfaction.

"There's our tree."

We stopped the car and scrambled through the thorny bushes that lined the road. The ground was hard clay with only burdock and weeds growing on it. There was nothing that would lead us to believe that any one had been there before. When we reached the tree, the coroner examined the ground around it carefully. When he arose he seemed disappointed.

"What did you expect to find here?" I asked.

"I didn't know what we might find. If the man who fired those shots used this tree, I thought we might find an empty cartridge or two. There ought to be at least some broken twigs or something to show that he was up there, but I find nothing at all."

"Still, the fact that the tree is where it is, makes the theory plausible."

He shook his head. "No. Now that I've seen how far we are from the road I don't think it does. Those bullet holes in the back of the car were fired from above and behind the machine. They slanted down but not sidewise. If a tree had been at the very side of the road, our theory would be acceptable, but if the murderer used this tree, two hundred yards from the road, he would have started firing before the car came opposite, with the probability that the holes would have been found in the side of the car. I'm sorry, for when I saw this tree, I thought we'd struck the right track."

"There's one thing I can't make out," I stated, "and that is the strange cry of my sister in her delirium. 'Look out, Jim! It's going to hit us,' she called out, and I would be willing to swear it had something to do with the murder."

The coroner thought a moment, then turned to me.

"What else did she say?"

"Nothing that seemed to refer to the accident. All the rest was apparently delirium. She begged forgiveness for some fancied wrong, and repeated that a certain man was not guilty of dishonesty. But her first weird cry had to do with the murder, I'm sure."

We walked back toward the road together. High overhead we heard the droning of an aeroplane and we both stopped to gaze at it. Suddenly the coroner clapped me on the shoulder.

"I've got it!"

"What do you mean?" I asked, bewildered.

"An aeroplane, man! Who owns an aeroplane around here?"

"I don't know. There are several at the aviation grounds. What's that got to do with it?"

"Everything! Don't you see? The bullets fired from above and behind. The number of bullets fired. Those two bullet holes in the foot-board of the car—everything points to an aeroplane. It was done a hundred, yes, a thousand times in the war. While I was over there with my hospital unit we used to get a lot of cases of motorcycle despatch riders who had been picked off by German aviators. They machine-gunned moving trains and military automobiles. It is one of the simplest tricks of a pilot's repertoire. Has Woods an aeroplane?"

"He was a military pilot in the French army and is the head of an aeroplane firm, but I don't think he has an aeroplane here."

"He could get one easy enough."

"The clever devil! Look over there! He had the broad sweep of the golf course as a perfect landing ground and this road hasn't a tree on it for a mile. He could have come down within fifty feet of the ground and followed that car, pumping bullets into it all the way. He had absolutely everything in his favor."

For a moment I saw red as I pictured Jim, helpless before approaching death. I could imagine Helen's agony as she saw that dim black shape come closer and closer and screamed in her terror, "Look out, Jim! It's going to hit us."

"Yes, but how are we going to prove it?" I asked.

"That's up to us now. An aeroplane has such speed that it was easy for Woods to fashion an ingenious alibi to account for every minute of his time on the night of the murder, but there must be some holes in it; there always is in a manufactured alibi. I want you to go over to the country-club and check up Mr. Woods' schedule of that night while I examine the golf links to see if he landed there."

We jumped into my car and drove rapidly to the club. I went into the house by the back way to avoid meeting people and asked for Jackson.

"Jackson, what time did Mr. Woods get out here on the evening Mr. Felderson was killed?"

"Ah espect he got heah 'bout six o'clock, Mistuh Thompson," the negro replied.

"Did you see him at that time?"

"Did Ah see him at dat time? Le'me see? Why, no, suh, Ah don' think ah did."

"When was the first time you did see him, Jackson?"

"Ah guess it was at dinnah time, suh. He was heah den."

"You're sure he was here all through dinner?" I asked.

"Yes, suh! He must hab been, 'cause he ohdahd dinnah."

"What time was he through dinner, do you know?"

The darky scratched his head. "Ah reckon it war just befoh he ohdahd me ter bring him dat drink."

"And he was here all that time?" I demanded.

"Yes, suh! He was right heah."

"Where did he sit?"

"Lemme see. Ah recollec' now, he ask me speshul fo' dat table ovah yondah by de winder."

"Can you find the boy that waited on that table that night?"

The old darky hurried away, but came back presently leading a scared yellow boy by the sleeve.

"Now, Geoge Henry, you-all quit youah contrahiness an' ansuh de genleman's questions o' Ah 'low Ah whup you."

"George, did you wait on that table over there by the window two weeks ago?"

"Ya-yas, suh! Ah ben waitin' on dat table fo' mo'n a month."

"Do you remember waiting on Mr. Frank Woods two weeks ago last Thursday night?" I asked.

The boy was trembling. He rolled frightened eyes toward Jackson who was glaring at him. Finally he broke into a wail. "Oh! Pappy Jackson, da's all Ah knows. He tell me he go to de bah an' ef'n anybuddy ask whah he go dat night to sen' em in dah."

"Just tell me what you know, George!" I said, motioning the angry Jackson away.

"He—he set down at de table but he ain't eat none," the boy stuttered.

"What do you mean, George?"

"He sit down an' look out de winder. Ah brung him some soup but he got up powful sudden, lak he had a call to de telephome, an' he ain't come back."

"Are you sure of that, George?"

"Yas, suh, Ah ast him did he want dinnah aftah he come back but he say he ain't hongry."

"What time was it when he came back?" I asked.

"Ha'f past eight, suh."

I gave the boy a dollar and he went away happy. Jackson had a sheepish look on his face.

"Then Mr. Woods wasn't here all through dinner, Jackson?"

"Drat dat boy, he make me out a liah fo' a dollah," he grinned.

"Are you sure, absolutely sure, that you saw Mr. Woods at half past eight?" I questioned.

"Yas, suh! You cain't catch me up no mo'. I saw Mistuh Woods at eight twenty-fahv exackly."

I handed him a bill and went into the bar. Grogan, the old bartender was there alone.

"Grogan, do you remember who was in the bar between seven-thirty and eight-thirty on the night of the Felderson murder?"

"Only one or two of the gentlemen, sir. There was Mr. Farnsworth and Mr. Brown and I think Mr. Woods."

"Are you sure Mr. Woods was in here?"

"Well, no, sir, not exactly. I remember Mr. Farnsworth and Mr. Brown. There were probably some others. The reason I think Mr. Woods was here was because he called my attention to the fact a few nights after the murder. There were a few gentlemen in here and they were talking of Mr. Felderson's death. Mr. Woods said, in view of the fact that the murderer hadn't been found, almost any one might be accused. Some one asked him if he was worried—we all knew, sir, that Mr. Felderson and Mr. Woods were not very friendly—and Mr. Woods laughed and said that fortunately he had a perfect alibi and called my attention to the fact that he was in here at about the time the crime was committed."

"And you're not sure that he was?" I asked.

"Oh, his alibi is good of course, because he was around the club all that evening. I guess he was here and I don't remember it."

I shook hands with him and left.

Far out on the golf links the coroner was bending over, examining something on the ground. When I reached him he grabbed me by the sleeve and pointed to two barely discernible tracks paralleling each other for almost a hundred yards. Between them ran a shallow, jagged rut, where the spade of an aeroplane had dug up the turf.

16

The Mechanician

W e've got it! We're on the trail at last!" I exclaimed. "I just found out at the club that Woods left his dinner hurriedly and was not seen again until twenty-five minutes past eight."

"We've got to go slow," cautioned the coroner. "A man who is ingenious enough to devise this means of murdering a man won't be tripped up for lack of a perfect alibi."

"I've found what that is too. He has the bartender at the club half believing that he was in the bar at the time the murder was committed." I told him briefly what I had discovered.

"See!" the coroner pointed out. "If they bring him into court, the bartender won't be able to swear he wasn't in the bar and the short time that he was absent will convince the jury that Woods is telling the truth and that our theory is all bunk."

"But we're not going to leave things as they stand, just when we are hot on the trail. What do we do now?"

"I'm of the opinion that there is a short-cut to the solution of the whole affair. Woods must have had a mechanician with him on the night of the murder."

"What makes you think that?" I asked rather impatiently.

"Because we know Woods came back to the club immediately after the murder and played cards the rest of the evening. He returned to the city in another man's car; obviously, then, some one else must have taken the aeroplane back to its hangar, since it would have caused too much comment had it been on the links in the morning. Our plan, then, is to find that mechanician and bribe or threaten him into telling the truth. If Woods hasn't got rid of him, he ought to be around the aviation grounds. We must wait until we are certain Woods is not there before trying to see our man."

"Then there is no better time than right now, for I know Woods is taking a certain young lady automobiling this afternoon."

"Let's go quickly then," exclaimed the coroner.

We climbed into the car and sped toward the city. Since Eastbrook is on the aerial postal route, we have a well-equipped aviation field just outside the city. Several of our younger set with special sporting proclivities have taken up aerial joy-riding since the war, so that there is always a group of mechanicians and hangers-on around the field.

I proposed to the coroner that we stop for Simpson and he agreed. When Simpson heard who it was he came down at once. As we sped toward the aerodrome I told him of our findings of the afternoon. He was astounded.

"You know, I'll hand it to the man who thought up that scheme. That's the cleverest piece of work I ever heard of, if your theories are correct and he really did do it."

"What makes you think Woods didn't do it?" I questioned.

"Not a thing," Simpson answered, "only I didn't know Woods kept a plane in Eastbrook. Of course, it would be easy enough for him to get one. Lord! Think of the possibilities it opens up. It fairly takes your breath away. Automobile bandits aren't in it. Imagine trying to cope with a gang of thieves who add an aeroplane to their kit of tools. Suppose they decide to rob the Guarantee Trust Company of New York or Tiffany's. The robbery itself would be the simplest part of the thing. It is getting the swag away that worries the criminals. Suppose they pull this robbery off and the police put a net around the city to guard against their escape. Mr. Thief and his gang sail away calmly over the heads of the police. Think of your diamond smugglers! Why, that big British dirigible could have flooded the American market with diamonds and laughed in the face of the customs authorities. I say it gets you."

"Yes, but in the meantime, we get Mr. Woods," I said grimly.

"Don't be too sure of that!" Simpson warned. "The man who thinks up such a scientific way of murdering people isn't going to be an easy man to catch."

Memories of big whole-hearted Jim came to my mind and I swore I would get Woods if I had to hang for it. Woods—murderer of Jim, after stealing his wife away, and now making love to Mary Pendleton, putting his bloody hands on her! The thought almost drove me mad.

We stopped our machine at the entrance to the field and walked toward the hangars. Three aeroplanes were out, being tuned up. They looked like birds, ready to take wing at the slightest disturbance. The coroner walked over to one of the helpers.

"Can you direct me to the hangar Mr. Frank Woods uses?"

"Woods?" the man repeated with a puzzled frown. "I don't remember any such machine here. I know most of 'em, but I don't think any Woods has a machine here. Wait! I'll ask Bill. He'd know if any one did."

He walked over to a group of mechanicians and returned in a moment.

"It's the last one down. He ain't had a machine here only two weeks.

That's the reason I didn't know the name."

We thanked him and started for the other end of the field. A pilot climbed into one of the machines. Two mechanicians spun the propeller and the engine sputtered and roared. The plane wabbled and swayed drunkenly out on to the field, then as the roar increased, it gathered speed and was off.

At the door of the Woods hangar, a red-haired mechanic of powerful build was cleaning and oiling some delicate-looking piece of mechanism. He looked up with a questioning frown as we approached, then became engrossed again in his work.

"Is this where Mr. Woods keeps his aeroplane?" the coroner asked.

"Un-hu," grunted the mechanician, continuing with his work.

"Mr. Woods isn't here, is he?"

"No," was the laconic reply.

"Are you Mr. Woods' mechanician?"

"One of 'em," the red one responded.

"How many has he?"

"Three."

"Are the others about?" continued the coroner.

"One of 'em is," said the mechanic, "and he just loves to answer fool questions."

The coroner laughed. "Excuse me, my friend, but I am in need of some important information. Will you tell me which one of the mechanicians was with Mr. Woods when he visited the country-club two weeks ago last Thursday night?"

The mechanic scrambled to his feet and advanced toward the coroner, his face twisted with passion. For a moment I thought he was going to attack us, but he stopped a foot in front of the coroner and snarled: "I don't know who you are, nor what you are, nor what you want, but I ain't no information bureau—See? So git t' hell out o' here if you know what's good for you!" With that he turned and disappeared inside the hangar.

We looked at one another. The signs seemed propitious.

"Would it do any good to try to bribe him?" I asked.

"You can try it if you want to; I don't care for the job," Simpson smiled.

"No," the coroner interposed. "He was with Woods that night and he won't talk."

"Shouldn't we get the police?" suggested Simpson.

"That wouldn't do any good," the coroner replied. "Wait a minute! I think I've got it." And with that he went inside.

Above us we heard the hum of a plane. We turned to watch it dip and glide and loop, in the afternoon sunlight. The sun, catching its wings, made it stand out against the blue sky like some fiery dragon-fly. It flew up, turned a somersault and nose-dived for a thousand feet, swung around in a wide circle, flew across the field at about four hundred feet, circled again and slid downward. Closer and closer it came to the ground, until the horizon was lost and it seemed to be gliding along the earth itself at terrific speed. Finally it nosed up, touched the earth, bounced away as though it were a rubber ball, touched again, and at last came to a stop within a hundred yards of where we were standing.

A girl climbed from it, and with a sickening clutch at my heart I recognized who it was. Mary had been aeroplaning with Woods instead of automobiling as I had supposed. At the sight of her, laughing gaily at some witticism that Woods made as they walked across the field toward us, my head spun with hatred and jealousy of the man.

I had no time to observe more, for there were angry shouts within the hangar and the coroner came bounding out, with the red-haired mechanician close behind him. The coroner had in his hand what looked like an iron crow-bar, and as the mechanician caught him, this bar became the center of the struggle. We hurried to the coroner's aid, but before we could reach him, the mechanician gave him a vicious kick in the stomach that sent him sprawling and helpless. With a curse, the mechanic picked up the tool they had been struggling for and dashed back into the hangar.

The coroner lay writhing where he had fallen, and could not speak. His breath was completely knocked out. We pumped his arms until at last he was able to gasp: "Get that——! Get that——!"

"It looks as though you had a little disagreement here," a laughing voice sounded behind us. "This isn't at all my idea of a hospitable reception for my guests."

We all turned to look into the smiling face of Woods. As we helped the coroner to his feet and began brushing him off Woods continued: "Gentlemen, if you are going to present me with the key to the city, please make it as unostentatious as possible." His smile still continued, but there was an odd glint in his eyes. Mary had left his side and was walking away. She had evidently seen me and did not want to speak to me.

The coroner cleared his throat. "Mr. Woods, I'm not here to make any presentation speeches. I am here to accuse you of the murder of James Felderson."

Not for an instant did the smile leave Frank Woods' face, nor did his expression change. He looked us over calmly and slowly and then he said: "Why, that is very interesting, but you seem to forget that I have already been accused of that murder once."

"You were accused on mere suspicion before, but now we have the proof."

The red-haired mechanic sauntered out of the doorway and walked over toward the aeroplane. Behind him followed another youth with a bunch of waste in his hand. The coroner pointed to the former.

"I had the machine gun with which you did the murder until your man there kicked me in the stomach and jerked it away from me. It's in the hangar now. But we don't need the gun, we've got enough evidence without it to convict you."

Woods looked us over carefully. He was by far the calmest one of the party.

"Gentlemen, I have already sent to the papers a statement that I am able to produce testimony as to my whereabouts during every minute of the night when James Felderson was killed. When the trial comes, I shall produce that testimony. If you think that machine gun is any proof against me, just step inside and I'll show you that it is of an entirely different caliber from the gun that killed Felderson."

We hesitated for a second, I think because of the brazen effrontery, the splendid calmness of the man. A doubt began to form in my mind as to whether he had anything to do with the murder at all. Woods noticed my hesitation and turning to me said with a smile: "Surely you aren't afraid of me, Thompson, when you so readily trust me with both your sister and your fiancée."

I longed with all my soul to hit the man between the eyes, to crush that half-sneering smile into his face with my heel, but I let the insult pass and followed the others inside.

"Here is the machine gun, gentlemen. If you will notice, it is a 36 caliber and not a 32 at all. If you will wait one minute, I'll get you the magazine. That will prove it to you beyond a doubt."

He left the hangar and the coroner picked up the gun.

"I could have sworn that the gun I had hold of was a 32. The barrel seems too small for a 36. Why, look here! This *is* a 32. Here is the caliber marked on it."

From outside came the sputter and crack of an aeroplane engine.

Simpson caught it first and dashed to the door.

"It's Woods' plane. He's going to escape."

We ran out of the hangar and across the field toward the aeroplane which, by now, was enveloped in blue vapor. Before we had gone half-way, it was taxi-cabbing across the field, careening first to one side and then to the other. Suddenly it swerved and turned in our direction. We stood there, a little breathless, to see what it would do. The engines of the plane droned higher as it came toward us.

Suddenly Simpson clutched my arm and yelled: "Look out! he's trying to run us down."

I ran wildly to one side of the field, not daring to look back but only trying to reach a place of safety. The sound of the engines came crashing to my ears like the staccato roar of a hundred machine guns. My legs felt as if they were lead. I seemed to be standing still. One frightened glance over my shoulder showed the machine, like some monstrous vulture, bearing down on me. I could feel it gaining and gaining. The heavy drone of the engines seemed to fill the air with its noise. A pitiful sense of helplessness gripped me. I knew I was going to die like a rat in the jaws of a fox terrier. I screamed aloud in my terror and pitched headlong on the turf. With a roar, and a rush of wind that almost lifted me from the ground, the aeroplane passed over me, its wheels no more than four feet from my head.

I am not sure to this day, whether Frank Woods tried to kill me or not. I don't know whether he was cheated of his game when I stumbled and the speed of his motor carried the plane off the ground, or whether he was just trying to put the fear of God in me. I will swear, however, that as the motor passed over my head, I heard Frank Woods' voice raised in a demoniacal laugh.

As the drum of the motor passed and I knew that I was safe for the moment, I raised my head to see if the devil should be planning to come back. With joy I saw he had risen to the height of fifteen or twenty feet. Suddenly the plane swooped up as though Woods were trying to loop. For a second it tipped sidewise like a cat boat reeling over in the wind, and then there was the sound of splintering wood and tearing silk, and the plane crashed miserably to the ground.

17

RED CAPITULATES

We hurried over to the smashed plane, the coroner leading. Woods, in his effort to run me down, had forgotten the telegraph wires at the end of the field. Too late, he had seen them and vainly tried to lift his machine clear of them. The wires had caught a wing and sent him crashing to the earth.

We found him underneath the engine, quite dead, the fall having killed him instantly. We made an improvised litter out of one of the wings and carried him to the nearest hangar. As we placed an overcoat over the shapeless form, I heard a sniffle behind me and found the red-haired mechanician at my side.

"You didn't get him, you dirty cops. He got away from you, after all."

"Yes, he's safe now," I murmured.

"Sure! An' he would 'a' been always if he hadn't been daff' over women. He never had no luck when he played the women. His takin' that skirt out this afternoon was what give him the hoodoo."

The coroner came over to him.

"Now that we can't get him, will you tell us about the night Mr. Woods killed Mr. Felderson?"

The mechanic showed himself distinctly hostile to the coroner.

"Oh, no you don't, you fly cop! Think I'll spill the beans and get meself in Dutch? You can go to hell!"

"I'll promise you won't be prosecuted if you will tell us what happened that night."

He looked us over suspiciously, but apparently reassured, he said: "Well, that's fair enough, especially since I didn't have nothin' to do with the croakin', although I know pretty much how it happened.

"The boss there come over to the plant—the International plant, you know—about two weeks ago and had me bring that plane out there over here. We always got along together, the boss and me. Wasn't pals or anything like that, but we understood each other. I'd seen, for a couple of months, that the boss had somethin' on his mind. I knew it wasn't any jane, because they never worried him none. He worried them a lot, but somehow he just took 'em as they come. He talked with me some—he claimed I was the best mechanician he had over there,—and I figured it out at last that what he was worryin' about was money. He spent a lot, an' was free an' easy, an' it worried him to figure that he was goin' to go bu'st pretty soon. The first day I was here, he brought a woman out, a swell looker—I didn't find out till afterwards that it was Felderson's wife—an' he kinda kidded her along about helpin' him over the rough spots by lendin' him a little of her dough. I sort of figured out he was goin' to run off with the woman, 'cause the next morning he come out and said we could take a month's lay-off if we wanted to, as he was goin' on his honeymoon. I thought he was goin' to take me along, but when he said that, I made up my mind to beat it back to the plant to keep from goin' bugs watchin' them other guys callin' theirselves mechanics, tinkerin' around them other busses when they didn't know their job. It's a darn wonder more of these fool dudes out here ain't been killed.

"Somethin' must 'a' slipped up, because he come out late that afternoon cussin' like the devil. He had one whale of a temper when he got started, the boss did. He took me with him in the buss and we cruised around the country for a while. Every time he spotted a straight stretch of road without too many trees, he'd come down and look it over. Finally we found that straight stretch of road out by the golf links at the country-club, an' that must 'a' suited him 'cause that was the only place we come to after that. He mounted that machine gun in there on the plane, an' it was then I decided he was a-goin' to slip somepin over on somebody. He didn't take me with him after that, but two or three times when he come into the field he'd swoop down on that there square target he made and put over in the corner and I'd hear the ratti-tat-tat of that machine gun a-goin'. I ast him what was he goin' to do with it an' he said: 'We're a-goin' out one of these nights and kill a skunk.'

"The afternoon of the night we went out to the country-club he come out here, kind of excited, but cool, if you know what I mean. You could see they was somethin' on his mind, but just the same he had his head with him every minute. Get me? He told me, as soon as it begin to get dusk, to take the plane out to the country-club and land on the links, about a half a mile from the club house, an' when I got there to flash my pocket lamp, until I see him light a cigarette on the club-house porch. I done as he told me, an' he come out. He wasn't dressed in a jumper, but just had a cap an' a rain-coat over his clothes. He told me to stay there, and after I started the engine, he streaked away. He left about eight o'clock and was back in fifteen minutes. He slipped me a fifty and told me to take the plane back an' to forgit 'at I'd brought it out. I ast him had he killed his skunk an' he laughed an' said, 'I made him pretty sick anyway.' I'd told the boys to have the flares out at the park as I was a-goin' to test the machine, so I didn't have no trouble in landin'."

He stopped and rolled a cigarette.

"That's all you know, is it?" the coroner asked.

"That's all I know, so help me Henry—but ain't it enough?"

He looked around at the three of us who had been listening intently to his story.

"I should say it is," said Simpson.

18

I Listen to My Forebears

Helen had come home. She preferred living with mother and myself, rather than opening up Jim's house, which she had been told belonged to her. Yes, her memory of past events was still gone, and each night I sat with her and repeated bits here and there of the experiences through which she had lived. Every now and then a thought would come to her and she would be able to fill in parts of the narrative, but this was seldom. In a way, it was fortunate, for I was able to leave out all the sordid details of her past and give her only the recollections worth keeping. As soon as she is quite strong, Doctor Forbes is going to reconstruct the tragedy for her, and he says he has every reason to believe that he will be successful in restoring her memory. In the meantime, she is entirely happy and content, and more beautiful than ever.

Mary had not spoken to me for a month. Somehow we could not get together. I realized how hasty and peremptory I had been in commanding her not to go with Woods, and I tried in a thousand different ways to make her realize that I was sorry. Whenever I found we were to be invited to the same dance or supper party, I lay awake half the night before, planning how I would approach her; what she would say and what I would say. It was a delightful game to play, because I always came out the victor. I made her say and do just the things that would make a reconciliation easy, but when we actually met, it was vastly different.

We were both invited to the Rupert-Smiths' ball, and I made up my mind that before the evening was over, I would be back in her good graces, on the same old footing. As much as I hated being treated like a younger brother, it was far better than being treated like a stepchild.

As soon as I saw her come into the ballroom, I hurried toward her, but at that moment the orchestra began a fox-trot and she whirled away in the arms of young Davis, smiling into his face as though she adored him. Davis holds a girl so tightly that it is actually indecent, but she seemed to enjoy it.

I was by her side, almost before the music stopped, but she turned away without looking in ray direction and, literally hanging on Davis' arm, made her way from the ballroom.

I finally caught her alone while she was waiting for some yokel to get her a glass of punch.

"Mary, may I have a dance?" I blurted out.

"I'm sorry, Mr. Thompson, but my program is full," she answered sweetly—too sweetly.

"But there aren't any programs," I insisted.

"Nor have I any dances left," she countered.

"Mary, I'm awfully sorry—"

"Oh! There you are, Mr. Steel," she laughed over my shoulder, "I almost thought you had forgotten me." I fled, leaving that ass, Steel, cooing the most puerile rot about how he couldn't forget her and so forth.

I called up Anne McClintock before the McClintock dinner and begged her as my guardian angel to put me next to Mary. She agreed on condition that she could put that Sterns woman, the parlor Bolshevic, on the other side of me. I consented, and through the entire dinner, Mary talked to old Grandfather McClintock about the labor disputes although she doesn't know the difference between a strike-out and a lock-out. She actually seemed perfectly contented to shout into that old man's ear all evening, though I did everything to get her attention except spill my plate in her lap. Afterward I heard her telling that Sterns woman what a charming couple we'd make. I tried to call on Mary twice and both times she was out—to me.

Finally people began to see that there was a serious difference between us and they avoided inviting us to small parties together, so that I saw her at only the largest, most formal and most stupid functions.

I had told Helen one day that I would be late to dinner on account of an important case. About three o'clock in the afternoon, however, I found that a certain book I needed was at the house, so I jumped into the car and went up after it. Mary's electric was out in front. For a moment I contemplated flight, Mary so obviously disliked me, but being determined that no girl in the world could keep me from going where I pleased, I trotted up the steps.

The door opened just as I reached the porch, and disclosed Mary hastily saying "Good-by" to Helen. The sight of her leaving, so as to avoid meeting me, angered me and some piratical old forebear of mine came down from above or came up from below at that moment and perched on my right shoulder.

"Treat 'em rough!" he whispered.

I hurried over to the door, walked in and slammed it after me.

Helen laughed and said: "Warren, dear, aren't you getting noisy?"

"Helen," I said, "will you please go into the other room?"

"Helen, stay here!" Mary ordered.

"I shall do neither the one nor the other. I shall go up-stairs." She turned to leave.

"If you go, Helen, I'll go with you," Mary announced.

Another ancestral spook with dwarfed, hairy body and gorilla arms, climbed to my left shoulder, sat down on his hunkers and whispered in my ear: "Treat 'em rough!"

"You're going to stay right here!" I commanded, grabbing her by the hand.

"Let go of my hand!" Mary demanded. "I am *not* going to stay here."

The sight of her sweet indignant face made my heart jump to my throat.

Helen laughed and went up-stairs.

"Mary—" I began, my voice softening.

My ancient forebears made wry faces at each other and hopped down from my shoulders.

"He's a fool!" announced the cave man.

"I'll say he is," answered the pirate.

"I'm not going to stay here a minute longer. Will you please get out of my way?" Mary said coldly.

"No, I won't!" I yelled. "I've had about enough of this, Mary. You think you can dangle me on the end of a string, like a damned jumping- jack, until you see fit to let me have a little rest."

My guiding ancestors hopped back on my shoulders.

"That's the stuff to give 'em!" yelled Hunkers.

"Treat 'em rough!" shouted Captain Kidd.

"You know I was right when I objected to your going with Frank Woods. It wasn't a friendly thing to do, after the way he messed up things in my family."

"Well, if you hadn't been so dictatorial—"

"Why shouldn't I be dictatorial?" I shouted, while my ancestors held their sides with laughter, "and this being my house I'm going to talk as loud as I please. If the girl I love, as no man ever loved a girl before, tries to go out with a man I think is wholly unworthy of her, why shouldn't I object? I'll do it again. I want you and I'm to have you, if I've got to fight for you. Even if I have to fight *you* for you."

Suddenly Mary buried her face in her hands. Her shoulders shook.

"Don't cry, Mary! I know I've—"

"I'm not crying, I—I'm laughing," she gurgled, dropping into a chair.

"Bupps, you do look so funny when you get excited."

I went over to her and made her make room for me on her chair, and then I put my arms around her.

"Mary, lover-darling, why did you go out with Frank Woods that day?"

"Why, Bupps, I was hunting the same proof that you were. I felt all along that Frank was guilty."

"I'm a brute!"

"You're a foolish boy," she said, twisting one of my few locks of hair.

She snuggled closer.

"Dearest of dearests, when are you going to stop teasing me?" I asked.

"Never, Buppkins!" she replied. "I just discovered that it brings out your strong points."

"Do you remember what you said when I tried to ask you to marry me?" I whispered. She shook her head.

"You told me to wait until Helen was well."

"You know, Bupps—the first thing I said to Helen this—this afternoon was—"

"What?"

"'How—how well you're looking.'"

With her face so close to mine and those lovely lips smiling at me so invitingly, there was only one thing to do, so I did it.

"The kid's got the stuff in him after all," said Hunkers.

"I'll say he has," agreed Captain Kidd.

About the Author

As part of our mission to publish great works of literary fiction and nonfiction, Colour the Classics Publishing Corp. is extremely dedicated to bringing to the forefront the amazing works of long dead and truly talented authors. Connect with us!

instagram.com/colourtheclassics

facebook.com/colourtheclassics

Milton Keynes UK
Ingram Content Group UK Ltd.
UKHW020745231123
433129UK00017B/1193